Red Somehow

A Premonition

Red Somehow

A Premonition

Joseph Musso Jr.

Published by
Goldfish Press, Seattle
2012 18th Ave. South
Seattle, WA 98144

Manufactured in the United States of America

ISBN 9780971160194
Library of Congress Catalog Card Number 2014957899

To Old Friends and Lost Places:

RED SOMEHOW
A Premonition

Down at the water, he is small. The ocean is big. Is where the simplest action exists: breathing.

Then one foot in the sand, then the other: walking. Until, footprints. Emerge.

In a LONG line.

They belong to no one. They belong to everyone. He stops, stares at the places outside of him, where the water swells. Is rough, yet gentle. Inside him, the simplest reaction: love.

Of life. Appreciation. Of the breath in his lungs, his eyesight, his hearing, his strong beating heart, his working arms and legs, his relative.

GOOD health.

And MODERATE age, not too old, not too young. I am in a good place, he thinks. I have lived, I will live some more.

Down at the water, roar, whssshh, mist, wind, sea gulls, plovers, time disappears or doesn't exist. Perhaps it only gets light and dark at intervals that are reliable. He wonders who decides what a day is, a year, how old am I really? Down at the water, there are no jobs. There is no money. There is nothing that money buys.

There is wind.

Birds.

Sky.

There is dream.

There is breathing.

His apartment building, beige brick, assigned parking spots, thirty seven apartments, his is number twenty seven, the day of his birthday. Through the window he can hear them. The waves. CRASH, crash-crash. On his balcony, small but clean, he can see them. Crash, crash-CRASH.

Outside and downstairs, on the building stoop, the door slowly creaks closed behind him. He stretches, notices a lone bird on a wire, balanced and still, its' only movement involuntary: feathers ruffled by the wind. The sea air, dominant, influential, is his to inhale deeply. He releases the breath, and feels clean inside.

On the boardwalk: the ocean closes in, bristles, twitches, snaps its teeth. Face to face with his own heart grown to immense proportion, he offers secrets, he offers memories, to the water, to the great body, which never asks in return, and always heals. How many others have cast their hearts to these same depths, cast their dreams, hope, love, their very lives? In what superb company I dwell, he thinks. To live among the sincere, the most earnest imaginations?

The first town, its wood planks, new. Every year, new. Coated, so feet glide, slide, skate almost, over them. Benches painted fresh, warm. Sit, they say. Drape an arm. Gaze.

Street-lamps, three headed.

Sprout.

From ornate iron poles, a flower of invention, blossom of light, a fragile hue, light-blue, drifts off petals when lit at dusk.

This light falls upon FACES.

These faces GLOW.

Each expression formed is an embrace of skin, bone, reflection.

Of light, both moon. AND man-made

Beauty is intimate. Between who, and who. Freckled white of a dandelion breaks apart at the gentle pull of breeze, the air now dappled with fragments of time passing. That moment, live that moment over and over or only once, is to live in the exquisite.

But an ODDNESS, a MOOD. Something UNDERSTOOD. Looks received. Looks away, looks down, disapproval, of his presence. The feeling of being TOLERATED by the indigenous people, an older clientele, belonging to a higher income bracket, is palpable. Thick.

In the throat.

Keep walking, keep walking, sand, sun, high school girls and the elderly patrol every entrance. No one gets on the beach without a badge or eight dollars cash.

Keep walking, keep walking, heat on neck, sweat, his face, palms, water, and water, and salt and grit. The bridge, stone and iron, a monument to function. He lingers at its middle, traffic GROWLS at his back. Leans over the old stone railing that has crumbled.

In spots.

But is not now.

Crumbling.

In spots.

And holds his hat because of the wind. Has lost hats before, because of the wind. Leapt from his head, soar, dip, rise, until landing at last in the choppy water below, froth, churn, gurgle, his arm still locked in place after having shot out in a fruitless grasp at air.

The canal, jetty rocks line each side. Between them the water chops itself up, the rocks black, wet, shiny, sharp, angular.

Waves leap over rocks, propel themselves, chests out.

Collide in mid-air.

Scatter.

Disintegrate.

Re-form and repeat, without end.

A fisherman, fishermen, in thin-soled shoes, careless or expert on the slippery rocks, bucket, pole, the man's wife, the men's wives, tying lines and pulling in, at line's end, wriggling.

A fish.

Small.

Barely food for one but in the bucket it goes. They work as a team, the couple, couples, silent and in precise repetition.

The sun, straight ahead, comes in like a train. When he lowers his head only slightly, the angle changes, and the ball of sun, fiery at its edges, has exploded. This explosion covers water, rocks, people, in a searing layer of yellow-red bubbling lava, the surface of the sun itself. The fishermen (glowing) (on fire) move among this, in their precise repetitions, unaffected, the tower at the end of the rocks continues to sway, waves continue to leap and churn, all inside this, covered by this.

Layer.

Then, another slight movement, he shifts just barely, up, and the layer has sucked itself back inside the sun, and the sun is a ball again, neat and packed in tight, fiery only at its edges.

He thinks: such slight change changes everything.

Boats motor in under the bridge, coming in from the ocean, in from the day. They head back to the marina, dock, dismantle their bones. They leave a trail in the water. An indentation that lasts, and is gone.

Now a larger boat, too big, it won't fit with the bridge down. So a signal rings out, red lights, gates drop. The bridge splits in the middle and rises in two separate parts. Equal.

Walkers, joggers, bicycles, traffic, waiting behind the gates.

The ship passes. Slow not fast. From a certain viewpoint only the mast is seen drifting by.

The bridge comes down, the split mends, and the bridge is whole again. The gates rise. Traffic goes. Walkers, joggers, bicycles.

Cross the bridge and a second town, this one different, this one swarming with lust.

College kids rent bungalows for the summer. The beach orgiastic with girls in bikinis, fresh skin, and bare chested boys muscled and tan, movie-star robotic in dark reflective sunglasses. The girls, college girls, their bodies curving around the world.

Also:

Volley ball.

Dive.

Miss.

Back on feet, brush off sand.

Also:

Frisbees.

Lazy tricks with fingertips, and behind the back.

Also:

Kites.

Traditional.

Elaborate.

Boxes, with tails.

Loop-de-loops.

The beach, ocean, boardwalk, the place where nothing is remembered or planned. The shelter of sanctuary. The great hiding place from a world in disarray.

Today it's the other direction. Instead of taking a right out the door, he turns left. And older planks, rotted in places, nails stick up, his shoe catches, he stumbles but keeps going as if it didn't happen, as if his shoe didn't catch the nail, because his shoe will always catch the nail.

The first town is.

Religious. Older than the others. A religious community. Retreats. And rallies.

For Jesus.

Tent City.

Pilgrimage.

Quaint shops, and cobblestones. Turn of the century houses with spires and high balconies, archways, and tall windows, row after row. The houses crooked but sturdy, crammed in close. No bars or liquor stores. Sunday services on the beach.

The next town is a small city. And as if a portal, he walks through the hollowed out Casino building, bustling a hundred years ago, only walls and ceiling now, bird nests high up, crows lined up on open window sills, a landmark, legend, and when emerging through the other side.

A different world.

Artistic and downtrodden.

He can hear it. Faint, at first. Music.

A drum circle, men in tank tops, dreadlocks, sweat, sway, eyes closed, stretching out the centuries. Hands move in blurs. It starts here, from this point, a groove, starts from this day, this time of day, this moment, a smile, a good feeling within manifesting itself in a deep breath released, and then another, another and another and another, tension pushed from the body, pulled out, released, gone, and what is left is that smile, one smile, the good feeling, a head bob, a foot tapping in the warm sunshine while people pass and waves collapse and the sun is a hot fist in the sky. And the drums, in unison, and his heartbeat is that small drum inside his chest, in unison.

Keep walking, keep walking. A man, fifty. Struggles. The guitar an unnatural part of him. Dylan songs, but only after a while do they sound.

Like Dylan songs.

Grits teeth and watches his chord changes, hunched over as strings.

Squeak. And fingers.

Clumsy.

Stagger down the fret-board, mash into each other, strangers, lost, confused, drunk.

A woman, brown skin, her afro a source of chaos, sweats through a tank-top, her face serious, her fingernails long, crimson. She takes turns: look at the man, look at infant in stroller: man, infant, man, infant. She protects.

Them both.

She says without saying: he is learning himself as he learns those songs. She says without saying: little one, one day you will replace him. I have to keep you both safe until then.

Keep walking, keep walking. Omar, old beard man, gray down to his stomach, black Kofi hat, tufts sprout from under, gray, ghost of Monk, ghost of America, ghost of New York City, 1941. Has tucked himself, beneath, for shade. A building overhang, still he sweats. Pours down his face. His trumpet breathes.

Out.

What's

In.

His heart, bleat, blech, bleat, blech, blech, blat. Harsh, eloquent stabs at the elusive truth of the Black man's existence in America, the attempt at diminishing Him, and His conquering of American culture. Bleeet bleeeeet, blapp bleek-bleek-bleeeeeeeeeek!

He leaves Omar for a bench in the sun. From there.

Is where.

He watches the man and his horn.

Lets his heavy head dangle free between his shoulder blades, and squints to see.

The magician.

Sideburns, bushy, white. Small wiry man perspires in the sun, in his usual spot up against the wood railing, near the ice cream vendor's cart, his magic top-hat pushed slight up off his forehead, beads of sweat get bigger, grow more pronounced, profound, kids make a semi circle around him, little girls in one-piece bathing suits, bellies, pigtails, little boys in trunks dripping water, skinny, bare chested, eager, sand in their hair: the kids squint in the sun and clap at the small tricks and walk off with balloons made into animals.

Candy.

Ice Cream.

A memory.

He stretches out on the bench, belly to the sun, one arm draped over his eyes, closed, the other arm, dangle, free, over the side. Here, there, he feels the slight warm breeze of a body passing.

He smells the brief fragrance when it's a woman, and the hardy sour musk when it is a man. When both, simultaneously, he can tell their compatibility by how well their smells blend or how badly they clash. He understands their complicity in all events that affect them.

Bits of conversation tear off in the breeze, attach themselves to his awareness, and then waft off.

He rolls onto his side.

The horn grows faint, then fainter. Soon, it's gone. The bits of talk, aromas, horn, gone. It's all gone. He's asleep.

He dreams vaguely, remembers little to nothing. Inside him wander remnants of a good mood taken back with him from his dreams.

Wobbly, groggy, hands in pockets, feet in disarray, disrepair. It's become cooler, because of the late hour of the day and wind off the sea.

One woman, and one more. Sit on crates overturned. Gray pony-tails, chains with medallions dangle between breasts that dangle too, natural, free from constraint, their smiles warm and, free from constraint, sweat at the armpits, neckline, faces flushed, women without married names, without emotional debt. They handle wood and string easily, small thin fingers glide, soft nimble thumbs, voices mingle, harmonize. This, inside the old Casino building, the building hollowed out, just the shell left, the guts long devoured by time, weather, city decay.

De Niro made a film here. Mickey Rourke.

Early in the century, men in tails, top hats, women in lavish dresses with hoops. Boardwalk casino. The olden days, in photographs black and white. The past is a place to live when here, when now, scowls too harshly. A place to think back to when what there is to think about today arrives in crimson and grease. So, photographs. Souvenir from the past, a reminder, a reason. Sacred. Pictures sold in boardwalk shops. Photographs without frames.

To jump into.

Where it's safe. Where it's simple.

One of the women plays a blues rhythm, while the other picks notes, clean, a slow lazy lope down along the fret-board. A man passes. He stops, smiles, lets.

A bill.

Drift.

Down, a feather.

Released from elegant fingers, the obedient fingers of a pianist, a man of music himself. And comes to rest comfortably inside the hat at the women's feet, the hat wide brimmed, red band around, upside down.

Pony Tail smiles at him, while continuing to play, while continuing to sing, her head rocks gently, her eyes nearly close, content, those eyes a hushed purple in the dimness of shadow, lavender, droop, the eyes, close nearly, lavender, spill out, the poetry of lessons learned, in life, over time, spill out of her eyes, she is mother, partner, musician, lover, and what is clear at this moment is very clear: What is contained in her eyes is contained in the man's eyes. What they share is having lived, heartbreak, children, loss, recovery. Swallowing sunshine, the medicine, a radiance from within growing outward, fill the body, senses, comprehension, counting lives, lifetimes, how many, in one, lifetime. He drifts away, and is gone, vanished but for the slight corner of a smile still lingering on the breeze, kicked into the air, a paper bag, that sliver of a smile, never touching the ground, romance, stranger to stranger, a love affair tucked neat and wordless inside the briefest moments.

Sometimes.

He watches the dogs. Sits on a bench and watches the parade of dogs on leashes and decides.

Which ones.

Are real dogs and which ones.

Are not.

That one. (a bulldog)

Yes that's a real dog, he's a bruiser, with soft eyes, and his balls hanging out. He's not covering up anything. He is what he is. Look at him slobbering.

It's decided:

The unreal dogs are the little ones that go yip-yip, puffy, curly, or shaved down to fit comfortably in the crook of an elbow – celebrity dogs. Yipping, yapping, tangled in the leash, trying to crawl up their owner's leg, shivering in the heat.

He loves dogs, all of them, more than people. Though for him there exists a kinship to the Labrador, the Shepherd, the Greyhound, the Setter, the Beagle, the Bassett, the Great Dane, the Saint Bernard. Also:

Any mutt with ooze in his eye and a rib or two showing, brings him to a knee, makes his arms wrap around. Also:

He will bring that dog home.

But this summer there have been fewer walks for him, less drum circles, bridges. Hardly has he ventured out. The last time, a month ago, at least, a long walk beneath a sun that was cruel. No cloud cover meant returning home with sunstroke, and two full days to recover, at imprecise intervals throwing up, a distant pleasure in an otherwise gritty oasis of misery.

For, at least during those retching minutes he could give in to involuntary action. He didn't have to hold back.

And so each day, as the temperature grows, he runs the shower, full blast, on cold. Twists the knob of the air conditioner in the living room all the way to the right (and the bedroom, too, in case a nap is in a somewhat near future). Peels off his clothes and slides under the water.

After his shower, a chair, a book. Toussaint.

Running Away.

Before that, Oster.

In The Train.

Before that, Gailly. Tsepeneag. Bataille. Camus. Rodiquet. Vi Khi Nao. Ourednik. Phillips. Crevel. Colic. Teodorovici. Saeterbakken. Tomin and then Tomin again. Seese. Kavanagh. Toussaint, Toussaint, again. Soupault. Bolano. Lipkin.

Henry Miller.

John Fante.

Before that, he is not sure. His memory is full of books. Thus, there remains room for little else. Forgetful, it is said. Scatterbrained. He forgets his own name. The way home from the grocery store.

If they only knew, the sheer amount of people in his head, stories, ideas, what those people say, what those people do. Empty out your head, I will empty out mine. A contest. Whose pile.

He finds himself creeping toward the smaller volumes, which in theory, but not always, make for the quicker reads. This strategy may at times give in to a portion of his anxiety.

Which then gives in to another portion: the need for more and more. Constantly he is on the search for another, unique, individual, a sea shell, rock, snowflake. Each its own. Its existence having arrived organically, its writer the same, both book and writer derived from a delirious if not perilous birth. The writer somehow saving his ideas to paper, and this paper somehow finding its way into his hands.

In this way, because ideas are endless, because books are endless, he is endless.

His name is Andrew.

Welcome to his addiction.

Never, for him, are there enough books. The more books he finds, the more he must find. Devours, devour. The taste of blood begets the taste for blood. Blood in a glass is called Cognac. His tongue swells, plump with flavor. No, a kiss. A kiss on his lips. Each book a kiss. Yes, that's it.

Today he will finish the Toussaint. And next, finally, Celine, perhaps the ripest strawberry. There can only be one first bite of the strawberry. One first delicious burst of flavor.

This one not a slim volume, this one thick with nightmares.

He takes a nap. He is always taking a nap. He wakes up. He is always waking up.

He takes another shower. Out of the shower and dressed, he pours ice water into a glass and sits on his black couch. Small couch, a love seat. Modern. His apartment is modern, all black and white, a photo in its negative. Black and white tables that curve as if they'd been heated to melting point and molded, twisted, smoothed. Also:

Black and white marble chessboard. Also:

Shoji room dividers, four and five-paneled, paintings, photographs, ten inch high statuettes of jazz bassist, flautist, heavy black iron, and, adding to the soup, his own paintings, which, as one can see, jut and ooze toward their own colorless destiny.

Em has pointed this out (non-judgmentally) (his modernity) while discussing how much she loves Shakespeare (did her Master's paper on him) and how much he doesn't.

Love Shakespeare, that is.

He says to her: I have tried. I have. but all that poetry you gush over does not move me even an inch in any direction.

Em says: well that's because you're a modern. look at your apartment.

Of course it's true.

For dinner, he eats candy.

From a box.

The kind given as a gift.

And drinks caffeine-free soda. The soda is lemon-lime. It feels lighter to him than cola. Cola has a foreboding element to it. Cola has a dark heart and wants to dominate me, he thinks. Lemon-lime however wants to pick flowers with me and do cartwheels down a grassy hill.

He thinks: I don't normally drink soda but lately I have the urge. I wonder why that is. is it the sugar? is it the carbonated roughness on my tongue? do I enjoy belching?

The phone rings. He answers with a mouth full of chocolate. Finally he swallows it down, washes it down (with flowers and cartwheels), and says hello.

On the phone:

His friend.

Calling from California, calling in fact from the busy corner of Columbus Avenue and Broadway, a corner Andrew has stood many times. He can hear traffic. He can hear the Chinese musicians.

His chest.

Hurts, and then.

Is hollow. A cavern he wanders.

His friend says: can you hear the traffic?

Yes, he tells him.

Can you hear the Chinese musicians?

Yes, he tells him.

His friend says: I'm right there. remember?

Yes, I remember.

He swallows hard. Wetness in his eyes. His chest.

Heaves. The musicians, old men, eight of them, play outside a Chinese restaurant. They sit on worn wood stools, expressionless, and play wood instruments that are hand-made.

A month earlier, Andrew had stopped. Listened. Breathed.

The traffic was heavy. Car horns. Trucks. He heard only the musicians.

A city offers its music free, and a walk through a city provides an education in the many styles of music available to the human heart, in its uncooked form, uncorrupted, unprocessed, music not made to be bought or sold, music leaving one body and entering another, entering through the tiniest contraption of all, the ear, an exquisite instrument itself, transmitting beauty in the raw.

His friend says, over the phone: the sun is shining but it's not hot. remember?

I remember.

He is happy. He is sad. He has the feeling his friend is happy, is sad. His friend says: you should have stayed.

He says: yes. I know. but circumstances.

His friend says: circumstances.

He says: well.

They ask each other the same question. His friend: when are you coming back? Him: when are you coming back?

The answer the same: well...

His friend tells stories, describes with great reverence the people he's encountered. Sitting in a bar at six in the morning, talking films, literature, sports. His friend's voice cracks with emotion. Films! he says. Literature, sports!

They hang up.

Andrew takes a shower.

In the shower this time the water is warmer. He lets the warm water skip down his spine. His neck cracks and tensions disintegrate. He likes to think in the shower.

Isolation.

The noise of water in his ear. Positioning himself (one step back) so he feels as if he is at the bottom of a waterfall, blinded by water as it splatters the top of his head and runs down into his eyes. In what he imagines as mad currents.

Never is he more at ease. Never does he feel safer.

Isolation.

Is not.

Desolation.

Soon Em will be here. She will be in my arms. I can touch her, kiss her, lay her down in bed. When she is not here I think too much. She will stop me from thinking too much.

He thinks: this is her greatest power.

He thinks: Minnesota is far.

He thinks: she looks good in those jeans she likes to wear. she looks good in that pink top with the lace, and the necklace, visible, barely, against her skin, centered, just above her breasts.

He turns the water hotter. Immediately shivers run up and down his spine. With a woman on his mind, his penis hardens. Since there is no logical reason to fight off perfectly logical urges, he makes a fist around his penis. He moves the fist front to back, back to front, in a continuous action.

Later, dried off and dressed, his flesh oozing inside the soft confines of the couch.

The apartment noiseless.

He finds myself staring thoughtfully at the blank canvas on the easel. The easel had been his mother's. Stored away for over a decade, he is happy to have it now, and paints furiously since its re-entrance into his life.

As a child, he remembers the easel, in the living room, always in the living room, sometimes in the center of the room, sometimes pushed off to the side, sometimes with a sheet over it.

In his parent's house. Her paintings. Not gifted. They are similar here.

He and his mother.

Her abilities lay in her tenacity. They are similar here. Her tenacity to try new things. She was an adventurer. He is an adventurer. They try things, do. Enjoy the trying as much as the things.

He likes the small items he shares with her, floating in the cosmos, caught in the gravitational pull of her energy and his. His only sadness: timing.

He missed it, when it was happening.

He didn't realize.

It was only later, after, that certain facts aligned with certain emotions, thus forcing out certain realizations from inside him. These realizations hovered in front of his eyes. For a very long time they were all he could see, causing him to marvel at his stupidity, colossal, really, making him wonder how he did not see them before. Often this wondering causes him pain.

The cruelest touch to life is often the lightest touch. How what is learned about ourselves, is learned most thoroughly after. After, he thinks. I learned more of life, the world, my place in it, after, and even later, when my father.

He thinks: I am out of parents – now what?

The lessons still come though. Recently his dog, ill, a decision. Never has he cried harder.

The lesson might be: stop loving. You don't get hurt if you don't get close. However, he prefers: love even more, harder, more intensely, less logically.

He takes a shower.

The blank canvas. For some time now he's had the idea. A new painting. Gray. No. Not gray.

An off-gray.

Gray almost.

A new gray, a gray never seen before.

Mixed with red, but only the hint of, the insinuation of. But not enough red that the red will dominate, as red is often wont to do, but instead red *flecks*, no not even flecks, but red somehow, *imbedded*, hiding really, peeking out, here, there, red not seen every time, only sometimes, in a flick, a flash, of an eye, of heat.

A gray created in a laboratory, after endless hours of mad experimenting. No, in a bog, with a stick that stirs up the mud, the mud clouds the water, a dew-drop drops from a tree branch, an auspicious branch, eager, stretching out into the world, from a YOUNG tree, with FIRE in its heart, the desire to reach, touch, feel, splash, the drop, and the clouded water dissipates. There!

Right THERE!

At that initial moment of dissipation, not a second before, not a second after. *That* gray.

That is the gray of the painting.

There will be three darker gray splotches/shapes (shapeless shapes, is there such a thing? does not everything have a shape? do I even know this, he wonders).

The biggest darker gray splotch/shape will be located toward the bottom left. Two smaller ones will appear elsewhere, one higher and to the right, and the other still to be determined. One of the smaller ones will be smaller than the other smaller one. One will be bigger. He wonders over these thoughts. Their sense, to him. They make sense.

To him.

As he stares.

The blank canvas.

Somehow a leg crosses over its other. And he sits like that. Wondering how long his hand.

No.

Not the hand, but.

Fingers.

Hesitant, curious.

Have been scratching his chin hair, the few scraggly wisps, and how long his eyes, suddenly feeling narrow, focused, zeroed in, have seen nothing but that blank canvas (not a single inch of the apartment around it, just the canvas). For weeks now he has envisioned this painting, this *gray*, but has yet to put brush to paint, paint to canvas.

He contemplates this scenario of incompletion, and, at the completion of this contemplation (for now), decides on more contemplation (in the near future). And so.

Still.

What??

He isn't sure.

But the canvas is blank. Still.

He walks outside, not in the street, but onto the balcony, and the sun, a demon in some cases, in this case, descends its heat upon him in an angry breath. Aiming. He staggers back, his entire arm sideways across his forehead.

Squinting. Squirming.

He leans over the railing, dangles his neck, staring straight. Three flights up, the world stares back at him. His superpowers are obvious: he can see long distances. There is haze, though. At first a film covering his eyes and he rubs them until they are red with sting. When burning, he stops.

No, it's not the eyes.

It's the heat, this heat, a weapon, biological in nature, nature's weapon. He decides to torture himself further, shades his eyes in a soldier's salute. Gazing. Skyward.

There:

A small plane buzzes, desperate, appears to be running out of gas, its sputtering engines clutch at the pale sheets of blue sky to pull itself along. Somehow the plane stays in the sky. Behind it, attached by long ropes or cables, a large banner advertises cheap beer at a local bar. He shuts the balcony door behind him. He takes a shower.

Later, it's dark, balcony door open, he plays his guitar, acoustic, cobalt blue, thin lithe body. The guitar is female, her temperaments, her curves and smooth fluid lines, the intimacy of a man alone with her, caress her soft neck, find melodies in her breath, and, the simple supple rhythmic truth of her heart beating against his fingertips.

When it rains, he falls with the rain, plays along with the rain, the rain another instrument, another player, and if thunder, lightning, then a band now has formed, of phantoms. The performance becomes more intimate, as the hour becomes later. For, as each man and woman in the world wander into the nocturne, the night is closer to being his alone.

When using a thin pick, paper thin, and with the guitar freshly tuned, and new strings, the sound becomes a jangly dream twisting both inside and outside the body. This is when he knows he is playing well: when it feels good.

Gary, a friend.

But is a friend a friend, when.

He berates you, when he sneers: You pick strings too much, too many notes. It's confusing. Look at me. I don't play notes. Also, that pick. No, no, no. Play with your fingers, your bare fingers. He insists.

Demands.

With, shockingly.

A fire in his eyes.

In Gary's trailer, next to the dog-runs, the dogs bark miserably at motorcycles in the distance, he strokes and strums. Gary, a new song. Andrew as audience is impeccable. Instinctively Andrew knows when to advance praise and when to hold it in reserve. He knows the questions to ask, and the questions to leave in the ether.

Gary enjoys the audience, revels in it, taking Andrew's praise when it arrives and pinning it to his face in the form.

Of a smile.

Broad.

They play together, when Gary teaches him a Patsy Cline song.

Not Crazy.

The other one. What is it?

Yes. Walking after midnight.

This, their saving grace. The one place. Where they play with precision, with joy. Here, there is no resentment that so often haunts their friendship. Here, is where the real friendship exists. Gary says, You need to start writing songs.

Need to.

You will.

When Andrew shows no interest, and may even have smirked at the suggestion.

Although not consciously.

Things between them, well. Abruptly Gary puts down his guitar. Darts, instead. A challenge. Dartboard on back of door, and the hallway long. The dogs bark still. Andrew, out loud, a question. Nope, Gary says. It never stops.

Are they ever let out of their pens?

No.

The dartboard. In the hallway, long. Where the bathroom. The bedrooms. Close the door and the dart board, crooked, on the back of the door.

Several games. No enthusiasm, trading wins. Then it's over. Music on the stereo. Folk. Then turns it off. Gary says, I can't listen to the radio any more. He rubs his bald head, makes the face, the curmudgeon, pleased with nothing. He says, The music there is dead.

On the back steps, they sit, top step. Gary built them with the simplest tools, his hands, what's in his head. With knowledge and wood. They smoke pot and stare out at the long dark field. Trees, slender and swaying. Moon, bright. They talk between long silences.

The dogs stop, at last they sleep? Andrew considers a latch without a lock. A simple action. An open pen door. The good consideration turns bad. The dogs run into the street, where cars are malicious, where trucks have no soul. The dogs are dead, or worse.

Still alive.

Twitching in the road. Confused. Terrified. Desperate to make a broken bone function. Bones and blood, blood and dragging, dragging itself, smearing a trail over the roadway asphalt.

And if the dogs survive the motorized world, how long before they starve? Where will they find food? Will they walk into a restaurant and order the lamb? Order take-out?

No.

Soon Andrew rationalizes the situation. At least they eat on a regular basis. At least they have shelter. And the latch remains latched.

Gary mentions poisoning them. A noble act, for the poor creatures' own good. But then a snarl on Gary's lips, vicious eyes, and the nobility descends to a far darker proposal.

Andrew says, his eyes on Gary: you mean your own good.

Friendships will last until one of them decides. Often, in place of love, like, friendship, in common, whatever. Is fear. Is lonely. Lonely is not your friend. Lonely is a liar, a trick, trickster, an imposter, a champion disguiser of emaciated emotions. Lonely will make someone look like a friend, when.

Andrew gathers all future words between them in his arms, and leaves the trailer. Gary, weaving his fingers, playing them in his lap, as an instrument, contributes his own silent disdain to the situation.

Outside, Andrew walks a hill, where his car sits cold and damp and spotted with cold beads of water. He is uncomfortable driving, even more uncomfortable at night. He thinks, out of breath: when I move to the city I will sell the car, or give it away. it has never belonged to me anyway. it has always been my father's. death signs no papers.

He thinks: in the city is freedom. buses, trolleys, feet. a bicycle. no. not a bicycle. a bicycle must be left places. outside libraries, bookstores, coffee shops, bars. must be locked, must be chained to something, fences, lamp posts, telephone poles, parking meters, memory. and the day I do not lock it is the day I donate it back to the universe. no bicycles. no possessions. just feet.

He thinks: yes feet cannot be stolen or loaned or forgotten.

In the car he shoves the gear-shift in reverse, steps down on the gas pedal.

And hears.

And possibly may have felt.

But isn't sure.

A thump.

The sound a body makes when thrown against a wall.

A man can be in his fifties. He can be in his underwear. He can shiver, bleed. He can be not quite seated, in the damp grass, but also not quite standing. Awkward and cross-legged but not completely, not completely cross-legged, holding himself up, but only partly.

Halted.

In time.

In that position.

A stop frame.

A man can be a photograph.

That man can have in his hand a can, open, of tuna fish, the lid attached but bent back, so the edges are sharp like a saw. Tuna fish juice, pulpy and white, can drip from his face.

A plastic fork.

The handle-end up the man's nostril, lodged up there, so the fork's prongs stick out. Startled, Andrew.

Stands over him. Startled, he.

Stands there.

Breathing out SMALL clouds.

The tuna fish, the fork, the odd position of the man. The quiet night now a series of faint drums, faint, familiar, inside Andrew's chest.

The car lights, Andrew's car, the one he wants to set free, like a dog, like the dogs in the pen, the car's lights shoot out a hundred feet over the circular dirt driveway, tracing that circle for a while before veering off into the grass. Two cylindrical beams, into the woods. The night breathes. Andrew can feel it, moist in his ear.

The drums.

Louder.

Too.

An uneasy feeling his stomach declines to accept, and repels. His nerves. He asks the man: are you hurt?

The man is unsure, confused. The man says nothing. Tuna fish on his cheek. Plastic fork up his nose. Wedged between a tree and a car, unable to sit, unable to stand. Andrew has described this to himself already. He describes it to himself again.

He repeats the question: are you hurt?

The man makes sounds this time. But no words. Sounds, noises seeping out from the unfortunate hole in his unfortunate face.

Andrew assumes shock.

Still, he has questions: why are you in your underwear? why are you eating tuna fish outside in the dark? do you live in that big house on top of the hill? do you live in the woods? have you escaped from a house of cards?

There is heat in Andrew's ears. He is waiting for some part of the scenario to make sense. He considers options. Before anything else he will need to see how badly the man is hurt, if he is hurt at all. Can you move, he asks. Can you stand? The man looks up. More noises, no words.

Did you bite off your tongue on impact?

Do you understand English?

Andrew thinks: did I just ask that? is there a dumber question to ask someone who does *not* understand English, than that, and to ask it *in* English?

He thinks: no. I'm not stupid. that is a perfectly reasonable question to ask.

He thinks: what is reasonable?

His car is running, the lights, the two bright beams lighting up the trees across the field. Are strong. Show no sign of weakening. Andrew puts his coat around the man's shoulders. The man shivers. The man's teeth chatter. Andrew checks the man's head, which is lopsided, did I do that, Andrew thinks, with the car? Did I make his head lopsided? Can that happen?

Andrew checks the man's lopsided head, the blood, which has stopped. He feels around the man's chest and his abdomen.

To no resistance.

The man lets Andrew do whatever Andrew wants.

He shows no pain, the man. No grimaces, or other faces, when Andrew presses here, there. Andrew says softly, relieved, to himself: okay that's good.

In the car now, Andrew turns off the headlights and turns on the heat. In the passenger seat, the man's teeth no longer chatter. Andrew keeps a set of clothes in the backseat: sweatpants and tee shirt. He puts the sweatpants on the man, an action that turns out much easier than expected.

The man still hasn't spoken and his eyes are calm.

Does he trust me, Andrew wonders.

The fork up the man's nose, now, this must be addressed, yes, that fork has to be removed.

This worries Andrew. He tries to judge how far up it is. How far up it has to be. To cause it. Brain damage. Can a fork handle, a plastic fork handle, cause brain damage?

If shoved up the nose at a certain angle?

With a certain force?

Is this that certain angle?

Is this that certain force?

Andrew worries. Maybe the man isn't talking because the fork has punctured that part of the brain which handles speech. Have I stolen the man's words? Have I taken his conversation away, his power of explanation, his small talk? His ability to sing, yell, yodel, charm? Ask for help?

Andrew is nauseas.

An impulse overtakes him. He grabs the fork prongs with both hands and yanks. It won't budge.

Andrew grunts. Makes a face. Plants a foot on the man's chest, who remains.

Docile.

Andrew is determined. He yanks harder, then grows terrified at what might be sticking to the end of the fork handle when it comes out: a bit of brain?

A small glob of brain, like a booger, at the end of a finger, after digging around?

Instantly Andrew lets go of the fork. Throws his hands in the air and backs away. At this point the fork slides out harmlessly. Andrew checks the tip. Nothing. A little blood, that's all. To be expected.

A hospital, then. That lopsided head, internal injuries, who knows. They drive. The man, in the passenger seat, stares straight ahead for the entire ride. Andrew parks, takes the man's arm, the man in sweatpants too tight, the man in a tiny coat, sleeve-cuffs nearly at the elbows.

Together they walk through the automatic doors of the Emergency Room. Andrew leaves the man with an admissions nurse.

Outside, clicking across the parking lot on his shoes, he wonders: should I have stayed?

Is this a hit and run? I mean, I have after all dressed him, in fact given away my own personal clothes, my coat, warmed him in my car, brought him to the hospital. I was even responsible, more or less, for removing that plastic fork. Aren't my responsibilities complete?

Andrew stops.

The moonlight gives him a spotlight.

A terrible spotlight where thoughts collide. Guilts converge. One of his hands involuntarily scratches the back of his other hand. He decides. He turns.

Inside again, he spots the man. Seated.

In a PLASTIC chair.

Slumped.

Alone.

Andrew sits in the chair next to him.

A few days later the image of the man in the hospital is still with him. Vivid in his mind. Is he familiar? Originally, at the edge of that cluster of trees, with the back of his car in the man's face, exhaust fumes hot, noxious, the man's face was a blur, a dissipating image floating in the toxic ether, nothing more, an amalgamation of others in similar situations Andrew had either seen in person or in films or conjured up in his imagination from the stories of others.

Is he familiar, though? In a real way? Do I know him?

He can't be sure.

The idea of the man's familiarity, him being someone Andrew knows, or had known at one time, or had met and shaken hands with, had smiled and exchanged small talk with.

Had.

Thus far, at least.

Refused to release its power over the obsessive nature of Andrew's thought processes. (And now it is entirely possible this image will haunt him, off and on, for a long time.)

He thinks hard.

He tries to remember.

But even when the man was in Andrew's car, dressed in Andrew's clothes, warming up, Andrew had not really looked at him. He only, well, a *vague* idea.

Of the man's facial presence. This, because, simply, it was the *entirety* of the man that Andrew had needed to act on behalf of, needed to counteract the seeming unwillingness of the man to survive on his own.

And, so at best, really, Andrew concludes. I only saw his face on the peripheral. For instance a quick passing glance as I struggled to get my coat over the man's trembling shoulders.

An effort such that it was the *shoulders* which held Andrew's focus. Each action went like that. The man's face was never the intended target of Andrew's look. Never had Andrew's full attention.

Even when addressing the plastic fork, stuck, the nostril. Andrew did not, even. For instance.

Notice the color of the man's eyes, despite the men being eye to eye, such was his focus on that fork, and pulling it out without any brain matter stuck on the tip.

Even in the hospital.

When Andrew went back inside, when the man was slumped down into himself, his chin pushed down against his chest and left shoulder, causing a severe smooshing, thus wrinkles, caved in face, crushed, distorted, what else, that Andrew never really saw his full pose. Smile for the camera! never came into play.

Even after the man had been given a small curtained off area in the emergency room.

While Andrew sat.

The small black stool that was supposed to. But didn't. Swivel, and when Andrew tried to swivel, the stool didn't move and Andrew lurched forward, hurting himself. Even then.

His concerns.

Were elsewhere.

Than the man's face.

Simply, it had not occurred to Andrew that this sorrowful creature in his, well.

Care.

Is the only word that fits. Might in fact be a long-lost relative, an uncle, Andrew's father, a much older brother cast aside to survive in the wilderness of an unsympathetic society.

After.

Say.

Serving his country.

Or the uncle, father, much older brother of his, or of a friend, or ex-girlfriend or some other (extended) family tree configuration, that, really, bares little to no edible fruit at certain crucial moments as these – Andrew thinks: what am I talking about?

The attending doctor.

Worn out.

His eyes.

Two black rocks weighing down the rest of his face.

Asks Andrew his relation to the patient. Who, the patient. Is now laid out flat on that uncomfortable ER bed, tubes running in and out of his nose and mouth and arm, wires hooked up from rips and tears in his flesh.

To several monitors, monitors that beep, squeak, burp, hum.

Relation? Andrew repeats the word. But thinks: hospitals. And shudders. Despicable places of horror. I will do my best not to revert to previous outbursts while mired in such dungeons. Certainly I have a history.

Yes, the doctor repeats. What relationship do you have to the patient?

None, I guess.

None?

No, none.

The doctor raises his eyebrows, writes on a clipboard.

The doctor asks the man's name, which Andrew does not know. His age, which again Andrew does not know. His address, his occupation, his place of occupation, his marital status, all of course beyond any information Andrew has gathered in the short time of his acquaintance with the man. He thinks: acquaintance?

Andrew says to everything: I don't know.

Then why are you here?

I think I hit him with my car.

You think?

Well, I was backing up. I heard a thump, or I think I heard a thump. It happened very fast.

Were you drinking? the doctor asks, terse.

Alcohol?

Yes, alcohol. He openly scowls now, the doctor.

No.

I see, says the doctor.

(Andrew sees no reason to mention the marijuana.)

Then the doctor makes another note, an angry scratch across the paper on the clipboard, then an angry click of his pen, and walks through the curtain, a third-rate comedian at the midnight show. The audience is stoic, unsure whether to applaud. The drinks are watered down.

Later, a policeman arrives. The policeman looks at Andrew. The policeman lets out a short groan, rolls his eyes.

Andrew stammers.

The policeman grabs his arm. Outside Andrew is asked questions, which he answers with remarkable calm, despite his earlier discomfort. After a while, he is told he can leave.

Feeling a responsibility now for the mystery man, and viewing this separation as a wrongful split up, feeling actual pain because of it, physical pain, in his stomach, his head, his chest, Andrew walks back inside the hospital, through the automatic glass doors, past the army of plastic chairs, past the admission nurse's desk, her head down, marking papers, then through the big white ER doors, down the long hallway of curtained off rooms, and re-enters the man's curtained off room, with, curiously, a certain sense of bug-eyed relief. Andrew's attempt, unimpeded up to this point, is finally thwarted, severely, by both the policeman and a muscled male nurse. It is then Andrew realizes that when the policeman said he can leave, what he meant was he *had* to leave.

Andrew's hysterical cries (with real tears in his eyes) does nothing to help his cause. Nor does the flailing of arms. Nor his feet kicking out in all directions. Just the opposite, all these histrionics only make his vanquishers angrier and more determined, thus justifying, in their eyes, their, what many might consider, accelerated use of force, for, it is true, that at one point, and for several dozen seconds, while being rushed outside, Andrew's feet never touched the ground.

Disheveled, exhausted, Andrew is deposited outside the hospital doors. He shoves his hands in his pockets. Shuffles to his car, where, he finds, disturbingly, two teenagers lying on the car's hood and staring up at the stars.

Andrew had parked on the street. The stars are bright. The teenagers are stretched out. They hold hands.

There isn't room for Andrew on the hood too. So, he sits on the curb, next to the bumper.

The three of them take turns pointing out stars. They each pick one, and then stare at all three for a while, then choose which is the brightest.

The male teenager says: have you ever gone bird counting?

Bird counting?

Yes. Bird counting.

No I have never gone bird counting.

The male teenager says: she's really good at it. go to the beach and count the seagulls. she counts them the fastest, whether they're in the air, or pecking around in the sand. she has a system.

The female teenager says: but you can only count the ones in the same batch. strays from other batches don't count. but even in the same batch every one is a little different. the key is finding the one physical characteristic they all have, and just look for that. you don't have to look at the whole seagull, that's how you make time. you have to study them. you can study math or you can study birds.

Andrew points in the sky. At a star.

He knows.

Is the brightest they've seen yet.

The teenagers stare at it too, for a long time, all of them in silence, before, with a subdued but very real admiration.

Agreeing. Yes.

That one.

The kids are gone. Andrew is gone. He drives. That vague familiarity again. Plagues him. Who was that man? If only I could have seen his face.

He pulls the car to a stop. He is home. He notices small dents in the hood, shoe heels, elbows. Star dust.

He takes a shower. He washes everything.

He takes a nap and dreams. He hears music throughout the dream. It is the radio left on. The nap is pleasant. Em was in the dream. She wore a quiet dress. She smiled and spoke poetry as conversation.

He feels lighter and jumps from bed. In his enthusiasm the floor acts as trampoline, propelling him. And he slams head first into the wall.

Crumples to the floor. Landing on a woman's shoe, a high-heel, extremely high, sharp, a weapon. The heel lodges in his back and the pain is an immediate enemy.

The phone rings.

Andrew cannot move. He finds this curious. He asks himself where did a woman's high-heel shoe come from? I don't remember a woman wearing high-heels in my apartment. Em doesn't wear high-heels. She abhors such evidence of expected gender roles.

The heel has wedged itself into his lower back, has somehow twisted through to his spine, as if being manually operated, punctured skin, and, when finally he manages to pull the high-heel from his back, has drawn blood.

Who left this trap for me, Andrew thinks. It's a mystery.

The phone:

It's Andrew's friend, from California. In his voice Andrew hears whiskey. His friend is excited and says he has been offered the backseat in a car headed around the country. Strangers. Brothers from Scotland he sat with in a North Beach bar for twenty hours. They said hop in Portland's next. They said eventually they'd get him as far as Chicago. Also, he met a girl.

Andrew says high-heels.

Andrew says you're not coming back are you?

In the morning Andrew decides. Yes a big breakfast. Sunday. Eggs, bacon, toast with butter *and* jam. But Andrew has no eggs, no bacon, no toast, no jam. Andrew has butter.

Andrew a few minutes later.

Downstairs, second floor.

At Gabrielle's door. Knock, knock. Knock, knock, knock. A man twice her age. In a bathrobe, in the doorway. He's tall.

Scratches his jaw, where a blotch, red, but not bright, but dull, scrubbed with dirt. Has formed. Not dirt, whiskers. Three. Four day's growth.

The man says: what?

He looks unhappy.

Eggs, Andrew says, caught off-guard. He had not expected anyone other than Gabrielle to answer. Bacon, he says.

Bathrobe shuts the door, without humor. Andrew feels foolish.

At a small convenience store Andrew walks the aisles. He has not washed his hair, so in all directions, his hair. Thus the baseball cap. San Francisco Giants. Also: he wears a tee shirt he picked off the bedroom floor. Also:

Flip-flops.

Also: jeans without a belt. So the jeans keep sliding down, which mires him in the endless process of pulling them back up.

Never do the jeans stay in place for more than a moment. He is caught in a time loop: pull up jeans, they fall, pull up jeans, they fall, pull up jeans…

While holding a carton of eggs.

A slab of bacon.

Loaf of bread.

Jug of orange juice.

Jar of jam.

And.

Finally.

Piping hot cup of coffee. Large.

At the counter Andrew unloads his bounty, pulls up jeans, yanks wallet from back pocket, with, it is unfortunate, too much force.

The wallet, then. There it goes.

Flying into the air, in a dazzling arc, sailing over the cashier's head. And landing.

Regrettably.

Behind the cashier. Behind the lottery station. Slamming against the wall of cigarets. And, finally, the wallet, flopping to the floor a wounded bird.

The cashier at first sleepy-eyed. Stares now at Andrew. Sheepish, Andrew makes a joke about not knowing his own strength.

Slowly.

Finally.

The cashier retrieves the wallet and, more or less. Slams it down in front of Andrew: did you do that on purpose?

I did not.

Because I'm not here to be your clown.

No, not.

Or your dog fetching your wallet.

At all.

The cashier stares, a long time.

The register gurgles and spits as the cashier angrily rings up each of Andrew's items. The cashier bags each item as he rings it up. The cashier mumbles under his breath with each item he bags.

Andrew.

Reaches into his wallet. Counts out bills. Not enough. He mumbles this terrible information to the cashier.

The cashier has a small forest fire in each of his eyes. His nose a steam engine. His mouth a volcano, about to.

Erupt.

Hot lava of fury. Furious words perhaps, but not yet. The cashier is silent, still.

A forest fire, a steam engine, a volcano, Andrew wonders…

Behind Andrew now, a line.

The cashier points a finger. At the end of the finger, a cash-machine in the far corner of the convenience store, by the toilet paper and cat food. Grace, Andrew thinks. And he, saunters.

With grace.

To the cash machine. His baseball cap. San Francisco Giants. Pulled down low over his eyes.

At the machine he sticks in his card, forgetting.

Of course.

The PIN number.

A horrifying blankness stretches across his mind. Knot in stomach, but, employing that grace again, does not show any discomfort. Instead, he pretends boredom.

When he glances at the cashier (the register, the items already bagged and the now nine people in line, and with all twenty eyes upon him), Andrew yawns.

He does not bother to smile. He knows it is way past that point now. He does, however, hear a man in line mutter that his coffee is getting cold.

While another man, with a newspaper, makes a remark about tourists.

Which at first Andrew hears as *terrorists*.

Andrew thinks: I most certainly am not a terrorist. Andrew is appalled, about to shout out in rage, before realizing the actual word said. I most certainly am not a tourist, either. Maybe he saw my San Francisco Giants baseball cap and thought.

Andrew pulls the cap down even lower, and, thankfully, remembers his pin number. Which he punches in immediately and with great relief and joy.

Finally, he thinks. Sweating. An end to this tiny nightmare. But, no, not so fast. Something's wrong. Instead of cash coming from the machine, he receives a receipt. On the receipt, it reads Insufficient Funds.

But that's impossible.

He slides the card through again, with, unfortunately, the same results. Crumpling up this blatantly lying sheet of paper and tossing it, with some anger, into the provided waste basket, he once again slides his card through. And. Again.

Insufficient Funds.

Again, crumple, toss, angry, slide card. At that moment, he hears a loud sigh. Glancing over his shoulder, he sees another line. They have poor posture, lean on one leg, shift weight, hang heads, hissing tires losing air.

Two lines now, Andrew is holding up two lines now.

He turns to the cash-machine line, tells them. One more try. I promise if it does not work I will move aside. Several heavy sighs, in flawless unison, a concert of them. Just as many shifts of weight from one leg to the other. They are a dance team.

This time the card works. Andrew takes his money, receipt, card, and.

Gracefully?

Saunters back to the check-out line. By this time all his items have been un-bagged and returned to their proper places, in their proper aisles. The line has moved.

Andrew speaks harshly to the cashier. His finger waggles. The cashier speaks harshly back. Their faces turn red. The decibel level of their voices rise.

Suddenly, Andrew.

Spins.

Andrew does not reach down a hand to the cashier. Andrew does not offer a towel for the blood. Before Andrew knows it, Andrew is halfway down the street. His hand.

Red.

At the knuckles, and.

Sore. Very.

Sore.

Home and hungry, he takes a shower. After the shower, having scrubbed away this latest humiliation, he reads in bed, in his underwear, shades drawn, door locked, the rainstorm CD playing in the CD player, and, after twenty pages, falls asleep.

He dreams of eating a vast feast, on a table as far as the eye can see. In the dream, it is well known that the table is a full mile long, crowded with food, breakfast food of all kinds. There are several men in the dream, and two women, and it is well known in the dream that The Day of a Mile of Food has been a raging success. All of them hug. We did it!

One

man

and

one

woman

yell out.

Hug, kiss each other. His hand runs down her leg. Her hand runs through his hair. Andrew in the dream feels jealous and hungry. These two conditions cease battling it out and join forces to make him unhappy. Abruptly the man and the woman are Andrew's father and mother when they were young.

Andrew wakes up.

He takes a shower. Andrew is not sure what the dream means. Andrew is not sure if dreams mean anything. The water is hot.

Hunger, though, persists.

At the drive-thru Andrew orders the Big Breakfast (eggs, sausage, pancakes, biscuit). He speaks into a small gray box. The small gray box speaks back. Telling him an amount. Telling him to pull up to the first window. He thanks the small gray box.

At the first window a girl with tinted skin smiles. He hands her money and says a hurried bunch of words. Somewhere in the hurried bunch of words is the word beautiful. She hands him back money and coins jingle while transferring from her petite hand to his large clumsy hand.

His car, idle. Fumes heavy in his throat. She smiles thinly, how people smile when they don't mean it. Her job is to smile, to trade money and to smile.

Andrew makes a motion with his hand, over his face, circles.

She stares at him, her smile gone. Frail, he thinks. No, delicate.

Andrew watches her. He thinks, soon, she will break. A figurine, of glass. Tinted.

He worries. Pretty like that.

He pulls up to the second window.

There, a woman not the first woman. Different. Her face carved. Rough. Andrew says hello. She stiff-arms a paper-bag out the window. Then coffee, stirrer.

Before he can grab the paper-bag, nearly he drops everything, but, fumbling, pulls it all inside his car.

The woman not the first woman stares. She shakes her head: that girl is sixteen!

Andrew drives out of the drive-thru. He considers. He pulls the car back around to where he first ordered, waits.

Patiently.

While a car in front of him orders, the small gray box, pulls up. He follows, until the first window again. He does not smile at the girl with the tinted skin and emerald eyes. She does not smile back, is nervous.

This time he does not tell her she is beautiful. This time he looks at her and makes a hurt face.

At the second window again. There, the woman. She is not surprised to see him. Her arms, folded, in front of her.

Andrew speaks softly: why is it wrong to say the word beautiful to someone?

The woman: you should be ashamed. sixteen. I told you.

Andrew: but I wasn't—

The woman interrupts: then what?

Andrew: then nothing.

The coffee, the stirrer. The paper bag of food.

He hands it back to her.

Home, he takes a shower, scrubbing off this latest episode, reads in bed, falls asleep, takes a shower. Andrew thinks: the water understands my need to be alone.

Em. She accepts my body, not as *a* body, not as just *any* body, but *my* body. She accepts my body inside her body, as part of her body. one body, our body.

It is how they talk while in bed, in melodies, in long slow ideas unfolding between them. The words do not hang in the air, around them, force themselves in or out. The words they say to each other are not their captors, do not trap them inside.

They are honest, in bed. To each other. To themselves. Outside, out there, in public, working, walking, on the bus, in restaurants, it is harder to be honest. They are different, out there. They are not who they are in here.

They try, but. Out there is not set up for truth. They try but become sad. They avoid looking at each other. They talk of mundane events. The weather. What should we have for dinner?

Andrew thinks: outside this bedroom, do we even exist as a couple?

As who we really are?

Do we exist at all?

Inside the bedroom, where hours and days will pass, Andrew is enormous inside her emotions for him. She, equally, casts her shadow above him. They are giants in each other's lives. And yet Andrew knows, at times, she feels small in his arms. She is easy to crush, so he must be careful. He thinks: no I'm the one easy to crush. that's why I must be careful.

Love is a word too easy.

To say, too hard to know what it means.

What does it mean? Love.

What kind of word is it?

What kind of word could it be? A word from another language. Old language from a lost world, buried under centuries of evolution, human development. A word made unfamiliar by its overuse, by its dishonesty.

Yes, he can say I love you, as much as they both understand what that word means. But that emotion known as "Love" has no word for it, not "love" or anything else. (Is "Love" the only word with such complications?)

He is happier when she is here, when she is happy. If she becomes selfish, then he withdraws into a darker world. He feels misunderstood, and trudges beneath storm clouds.

He feels betrayed, no, not betrayed. He feels insignificant, because she has lost interest in him. Traded it for interest in herself.

Neglected.

Andrew thinks.

Means.

Betrayed.

Selfish, he thinks. Which one of us, then, is that?

But when she is generous with her attention, her affection, with her body and her mind, he is safe. Without her, often he is restless, fearful. The world becomes a place of sharp edges. The buildings have spurs on them. Lamp-posts have razorblades glued on. Small daggers travel the wind.

And.

So.

His clothes get caught. He cuts easily. Words injure him, the words of strangers. Looks puncture. Laughing, must, just must, be aimed at him.

Andrew walks out on his balcony. Midnight. No. Well past. A rustling. It's the garbage dumpster.

Squirrels.

Feasting in peace. No, not squirrels.

The head of a man. Very quiet (or attempting to be very quiet). A man.

In a certain process.

In the process of climbing.

Climbing inside the dumpster, nestling in with the trash, cuddling it.

It's cold tonight, the man says in Andrew's apartment. He rubs his palms together briskly enough. To start a fire. Not Andrew, the other one. Andrew is not sure, maybe. Is this the one I hit with the car? No.

But is he?

Andrew brings tea.

The man says: trash. He says: trash is warm. also it's amorphous, so it clings to you, fills in around you good. gets into your empty spots and packs you in, takes on your shape. you can survive the night but you have to give in to it. you have to accept the idea of being part of the trash, being the trash itself. plus the walls of the dumpster keep out the wind. and if it rains, you can flip over the rubber tops.

Andrew feels this is reasonable.

Andrew has very little food in his apartment. Gives the man what he has. There is peanut butter and jelly. Single slice of bread.

End piece.

In rolled up plastic bread bag without twist-tie.

One beer in the fridge. Milk, expiration date is hieroglyphics. It has a.

Crust.

On top. The milk.

And a smell.

The man looks at Andrew.

Andrew shrugs: I'm afraid of it.

Andrew says: do you want the beer?

The man says: beer is a sad dream. one makes you want more, more than one makes you do things you wouldn't normally do.

Andrew asks: did I hit you with my car?

They run the tap in the sink, drink water, no ice cubes. The trays are empty.

Were you, the man asks.

Andrew: what?

Planning on it?

Andrew: why would you say that?

Because you keep the food of a man not expecting to be here tomorrow.

Andrew: I live day to day. a choice.

Whose choice, the man says.

The man has a look on his face, skepticism. Lemons. As if sucking on. Lemons.

He watches Andrew. Andrew's plain existence, the emptiness, the hollow apartment. The panting walls and bad-breath curtains. This depresses Andrew, this watching. Am I living in a garbage dumpster too? Is this what he sees? Andrew's head slumps. His feet paw the rug. Until the man with his eye roaming the apartment arrives at the.

Books.

So many books.

Andrew's books. Arranged is not the word. On the floor, slapdash. A pile finds its own structure. A pile is a structure.

The man, his face split by a smile. Falls to both knees, handles the books, as skin, as rare bits of cloth, a scarf, silk, running through his fingers. The lemons are gone.

In rapture, the man. Broadly, insanely. Smiling.

Holds the cloth up to his face, a book, rubs against his cheek.

Words!

It's the man, bellowing. Thought!

With both hands, he thrusts a book high in the air. Trembles.

Then no more, there are no more words from him, because action has taken control of him, and he, dives, head-first into the raked-leaves pile of books. He rolls around in them, picks them from his hair, mouth. Leaves. Books. A childhood. An innocence.

On his knees, his coat off now, thrown off, strewn on the floor. In a fever that is senseless. Haste and urgency burn off his fingertips. Steam. He takes a book like a man takes a woman. Bataille, Breton, Miller, Cocteau, Sartre, de Beauvoir, Camus, Soupault, Crevel, Barbusse, Aragon, Nin, Unger, Leve, Basara, Celine. Breathes against it. His lips turn pages. He is beside himself. One after another he opens a book to its middle, devours the words, in silence, lips move, flutter flutter the eyes, his expression of, again, yes, rapture.

What better woman than literature! It is the man, yet crazed, sweat, bellow, again. Fling his lungs around the room, bounce them off the walls. Rebound, resound. What better meal! What better feast! He is tall, the man, six and a half feet, long legs, long hair, gray, knotted, he raises another one high in the air, one hand, thrusts it, on his face now a contorted look, radical, fearless, audacious. A young priest with his bible out to prove God.

> This!
>
> The man, he says.
>
> He says loudly: this!
>
> This is my weapon. How I protect. Me. From. All of it.
>
> He says: my enemies shrink in the shine of this great weapon in my hand! the blinding luster of *ideas* burning holes in their flesh, protects me, stultifies the great army impeding me, puts them down in the very valley which WAS to soak with my blood, while NOW I gallop through them untouched!
>
> He says: ideas! it's ideas that fall in love. men and women, no, never. but the ideas men have, the ideas women have, it's the ideas which embrace, which

fulfill the flesh! which penetrate! which accept the penetration!

The poetry of his outburst affects Andrew. His chest, slightly.

Heaves.

His heart races.

The man is in the shower. Andrew feels worried. He is not comfortable with others in his sanctuary. The man, his clothes wash in the basement laundry room. The same size.

Roughly.

As Andrew.

Andrew picks out jeans, tee-shirt, heavy flannel shirt, socks, boots.

Later, in silence, the old clothes are transferred to the dryer. The man, dressed now in Andrew's clothes. They walk the beach, down by the water. The Soupault tucked under his arm.

They don't talk. The water is loud and speaks for them. The darkness, without a visible moon. They are tired but exhilarated.

The man asks Andrew what he does during the day. Andrew ponders. Horrible things, Andrew says. I.

Work.

Andrew is ashamed.

A perilous activity based in mindlessness.

But you make money, the man points out. For roof.

I have traded my health for that roof.

You're ill?

Of heart.

But the books!

Yes they sustain me.

What of a woman?

She is far away.

Where is she?

Buried in my dreams.

Mine is buried in the ground. Often, we only get one, so be careful with yours. Some break easily. Some break you.

They stumble, amble toward nowhere, the shushing lullaby of feet into sand. The soft noise of water. And the moon, a slightness in the sky, its presence vague.

Makes the narrowest path of light in the dark sand. Both, they stagger, crooked, inside the lines, inside the path of light, for a moment, heading, to, then outside, re-appearing, disappearing, by the step, half in, half out, of existence.

Back in Andrew's apartment, without asking, the man picks up Andrew's guitar. The acoustic. Blue. Cut from the sky. And begins to, loud, play and sing. Joyful, the man, his eyes. Close.

Andrew pictures a backyard wedding.

Guests, their ramshackle suits and country Sunday-best dresses burst from their bodies, the bodies themselves oiled with sweat, the sweat from constant movement, constant dance, eat, drink, loud sweaty muss-haired open-mouthed talk in the sun and sticky air of swamp and brush.

He pictures a young man and woman, repeat words they have only, heard, before. Have yet to live. How they mistake promises for prayers.

Then he ERASES these images from his mind, even scrape the blackboard with fingernails, to chase off images.

No. This would be no wedding music. The energy is wrong.

Yes the man plays and sings, stomps quality. Foot large, heavy, up then down, full smile, his beard desperate, in delirium. Beard LEAPS from and comes back TO his face.

In that moment clean-cut, soft, safe, the mask dissolved. But, then.

Snap!

The whiskers back in.

Place. Snap!

The man back in.

Place.

Andrew wonders: my downstairs neighbor. is it too loud? will she mind?

He thinks: Gabrielle? will he, that new one?

Hardly have they talked at length throughout the years, Andrew and Gabrielle. Yes at times, small talk. Words near invisible and useless. Such obligation a heavy shadow on certain shoulders. Andrew shudders: what a disgraceful attempt at human communication, this small talk, a thief, a pick-pocket, stealing what is real! small talk is a crime of the heart, an execution of the soul.

And yet at times.

Necessary.

To escape unfamiliar faces, uncomfortable situations.

A few words of the weather, timed correctly, and both walk away convinced of the other's pleasant nature. One night, though, she cries in the laundry room.

Andrew has just entered, weighed down with basket, full, every item of clothes he owns, but for what he wears. Piled high. In a mound.

In her apartment, she tells Andrew about her boyfriend. Left after thirteen years together. She says the words career and jealously.

Outside on her balcony, she says again the word jealousy. She and Andrew sip beers. Small metal table, round, flimsy, tied with cords to the railing because of the wind-storms. It begins to rain.

Melancholy.

She reports: I was with him for twenty years, living together for thirteen. I've known no other man.

And he left, she continues, astonished. Because he didn't want a commitment. What did he think thirteen years was?

The ocean. White-caps. Whoosh and swooosh. Crash, psshhh. What is beautiful once can never be beautiful again.

She says: what?

Andrew says: nothing.

She says: no, what?

Andrew says: it's the basic principles of beauty. once beauty is gone, it's gone forever. the relationship between a person and what they see as beauty cannot last beyond that moment of first realizing the beauty. the person can appreciate the beautiful thing the rest of their life, but that is appreciation of the thing and not the thing itself. beauty was never meant to live much past its birth.

She is not sure what he means. Her face reveals this, confusion. She says, You bump into furniture when you talk.

Soon, the subject changes. They talk books, music. Her taste runs toward the popular, while, Andrew, no, not the popular, but the opposite. She is intelligent, honest, a psychologist.

Time passes, they talk, laugh.

He isn't sure. He says: is this a session? are you my neighbor or my doctor?

Yes, she says to his questions.

I hear you playing, she says. Smiling, her cheeks full, rosy from the weather. Andrew blushes. He is not sure why.

He does not feel desire.

He tells her about Em. A long distance relationship, he murmurs as if it is an ugliness. And says: is absence an aphrodisiac or just impossible?

The wind picks up. Raindrops, a few, sneak in, prick gentle his skin. But. No. That's all.

She tells Andrew: I'm probably out here more when there's a storm than when it's sunny out.

Andrew says: your hair is red.

Yes.

He says: isn't that supposed to mean something?

She says, Do you think it means something?

Andrew says: is this your office or are we on your balcony?

Often, in the night, sirens, scream, gurgle. The window is open, the balcony door. Andrew wonders who is chasing who, who is bleeding somewhere. Who is running off. Some nights he doesn't hear them.

Andrew thinks: often, when a person I will never see again mentions the weather, I tell them I hear sirens. I tell them I try to follow the sirens with my ear, but get lost in the side streets of my imagination. everything should have a point. and when it doesn't, I get lost in my imagination.

The man plays the guitar, sings, stomps.

In the morning Andrew takes a nap. He takes a shower. He reads in bed. He takes a nap. He wakes up.

The man, Theodore. Makes eggs. At the stove, a spatula. Sizzle. Shhprrt. Coffee. Here, he says, holding out a mug. Andrew takes it.

Theodore comes and goes. Now he is gone. The couch was made up. Now blanket and sheet sit folded at the end of the couch, neat, a pillow, flat, airless, on top.

Andrew in the shower, a knock on the front door. He steps out of the shower, leaves it running. He walks to the door. He opens the door.

 Pete.

 Greta.

 Andrew lets them in.

 Pete says: you're naked.

Moments later, Andrew returns. Jeans, tee shirt. Bare feet. Hair wet. He has shut the shower off.

Pete in the white chair. Greta on the black couch. Andrew thinks: opposites.

He offers drinks: I have scotch, a Christmas bottle I found this morning. no beer though. the last one was drunk by what may have been a hallucination.

A hallucination? Pete asks.

I often do not feel real, Andrew says.

Water, Greta says meekly. Is fine. Her shoulders are hunched, poor posture. A withered tree, Andrew thinks. Her eyes, always dark, big, remain so now, but now they are the most of her. The rest of her is disappearing. Her bones stick through. Shoulder blades sprout from her back like wings. She has lost weight, too much. Herself, too much.

Greta her water, Pete, scotch. Andrew squats on the rug. The balcony door is open and a slight pleasing breeze enters the apartment, lingers just long enough for the next one to arrive. This is how it gets cold. The air collects.

It is not cold.

Pete makes a remark. While he eye the glass, holds it up and tilted. So a triangle of liquid occupies the bottom corner of the glass. Ah, I see you still drink the good stuff.

Andrew: it was a gift.

Greta is quiet. It bothers Andrew. She sips the water with guilt.

Pete admonishes her and calls her a name.

Greta, her head drops. She holds the water glass in both hands. The hands are purple. She holds the glass tight, the hands stretched, fingers web like. Bony. No verbal reply, this is her reply. The hands.

Like this.

Pete looks back at Andrew. Shakes his head.

Andrew is confused. She drinks a glass of water. What is unreasonable here?

Pete sips his scotch.

Carrots. Pete crunches them in his teeth.

It's all I have, Andrew says. Frowns.

Not at all, they're good. Healthy. Ah, yes! We should all eat more carrots and see for miles! Yes!

Greta, Andrew says, and offers the plate. She remains motionless as Pete pushes the plate back at Andrew, says she's eaten enough for one day.

Andrew: but it's early.

Pete, stern now: she's not hungry.

Greta is a painter, turning paint into voluptuous renditions of men and women embraced in desire.

Another item of information about her is, with just enough wine in her, and the proper encouragement at this or that party, she will stand up and sing with flawless clarity and pitch. She is easy to talk to, and although quiet, shy even, she possesses a profundity about life, her charm a lure, a charm as subtle as lace, as supple as the flesh of brilliance.

Andrew thinks: this is not her. today is not her. things have gotten out of hand.

Andrew stands up, orders Pete from the apartment. Greta, Andrew says. You can stay.

Greta does not stay.

Before leaving, Pete smashes an ash tray to the floor. Bored, Andrew allows it. Pete stands in front of Andrew. They are eye to eye. Pete's face is.

Vivid.

Bright and bursting.

Both his hands ball into fists. They hang, the fists, as weapons. Ready.

Now the fists.

Bang against his legs.

Pete stares a long time. Bored, still, Andrew.

Again.

Says: get out.

Andrew, again: Greta...

He notices now. He did not before. A mark. Greta declines, follows Pete out the door, her shoulders hunched.

Her head down.

In her blind scurrying, she bumps into Pete's back. Pete twirls, his rage meant for Andrew. Perhaps one of his fists raise, perhaps it doesn't. Andrew and Pete, their eyes.

Silence.

Jaws set.

Silence.

Muscles tense.

Silence.

Motionless.

Pete leaves.

Andrew thinks: I can't vouch for what will happen outside my apartment door, but it will not happen inside it.

Andrew on the balcony. Refuge. He rubs his temples until he can feel his eyes in his fingers. He closes and opens his hands three times. A very good feeling, this release of tension the eyes hold. Andrew feels the stresses drift out and away from him. He can see them in the air.

Vanishing.

This is the discarded part of him, not really a part of him, but a part others have attached to him. He is thankful to pry it loose. He is thankful to shed those negative layers. He is thankful when they blow out to sea.

When people damage him he is loud inside.

He feels quiet and peaceful now.

A garbage truck arrives. It feels like an abrupt arrival. Noise and stench and barge right in.

Man inside seems to have no bones in his body. Andrew thinks: is this what relaxed looks like? like having no bones in your body?

Man works alone.

In jeans.

Sweatshirt.

Ear-covering hat.

Gloves that might be oven mitts.

Hook the dumpster with rubber straps, secure it, test by pulling. Then, a lever. The dumpster in the air now, hover over truck. Punch red button big as his fist. Dumpster, whir and grind. Tips upside down.

The cohesion of falling objects, the simplicity of one after another, the tumbling blur of it all at once. He wants it to keep going. He feels happy and content. He feels like there are no bones in his body.

Mechanical, musical, industrial grind and crunch and whir and squeal. The noise is warm and Andrew gets chills that are warm. The kind he has climbed inside of before.

He empties himself like that, too, all debris, all at once.

That ground floor apartment, when he turns. The empty one with the fight and blood and tenants kicked out.

Workers renovate and scrub.

Open window – a radio. Static. Crash of metal brackets through the window, onto the asphalt. Tinnngggggggg! Reverberate, and jangle. Such melody, Andrew.

Hears melodies. All day, Andrew hears.

Melodies. They melt into crystal pools inside his head.

A kid, twenty, filthy face and hair and shirt and jeans. Sag, the jeans. Pant legs bunch at boot tongue. Boots scuff ground, drear, exhaustion, feet too heavy to pick up and put down.

Drag broken sheetrock across parking lot. Crooked white lines from the scrape. A trail without tom-toms, winding, so he can find his way back, for more.

Tersshhhhh, the sound of sheetrock dragged. The song. And then, lift. Heave. Thump-whoosh into the dumpster, empty again, but not for long. Dust shoots out.

Pipes, next. The kid inside the empty apartment throws pipes out next. The kid outside drags pipes to the dumpster. Plumbing pipes click clack jingle jangle ting. Sound of change in a pocket, sound of bells in the barn. Andrew, his eyes.

Close.

For sleep.

A buzzing, not close, but far off. Not a plane. A drill maybe. Neither, maybe. What, then? Andrew thinks: I don't need to know. I don't need to know everything.

Breeze, slow, soft, lopes in from the ocean, muss the hair of trees. The trees sway, just a shiver, a quiver when touched tenderly. Bird on a branch feels the light vibration and wiggles its feathers and lets out a chirp. Andrew, dreamy, mumbles: I am relatively healthy. I will never complain. I have lived. I will live some more.

Dan. Andrew's neighbor, next door. Teacher.

High school.

A woman. One Andrew hasn't seen before, walk across the parking lot. Andrew watches them from his balcony, where often he is invisible. Dan's last woman moved out. Andrew saw her in the hallway after her workout. She was sweaty. She smiled. She had never smiled at Andrew before. She'd decided.

Dan.

Not long after, she was gone.

Dan.

His shaved head inappropriate for his body-type. No, not inappropriate. The wrong word. What is the word? Andrew thinks: I don't know the word. but his body is soft, not obese but soft, chubby. His face, too. No, not chubby. Oh I don't know.

Andrew knows him as someone who stays up all night, someone intelligent, eccentric, but only slightly. And.

Also.

Nice enough in every general way.

Severe fan of American football, a trait which in most has in the past caused Andrew to question that person's intelligence but in Dan he writes off as aberration.

The woman Dan walks with is plain in the face, pudgy, about Dan's age.

Kindly looking.

Her stride.

Confident.

Had they met the night before, a bar? Had she come home with him? And now he walks her to her car?

They chat as they walk. Andrew watches each new step they take with greater interest. He has followed the storyline this far. Now they.

Kiss.

At her car.

Not passion.

But on the cheek, a peck. Despite where their mouths had been the night before. That was the night before.

They smile.

She climbs down into her car, a practical model painted a practical color. Starts up the engine. Andrew hears the soft purr and enjoys the smooth soothing sound of the engine. His chest is quiet. Sleep is soon.

Slowly, she backs out of the parking space, changes gears, and moves the car forward. Dan, hands in pockets, now, watches until her tail-lights descend the slightly elevated parking-lot driveway and disappear down the street. He frees one hand in order to toss out a small wave. He walks back, the hand returned to his pocket.

When Dan is gone the old man with the bright fancy sports-car appears. The old man takes up more of the parking lot than Dan and the woman. The parking-lot can hardly hold him. He needs all of the space available. A sideways walk, an amble nearly, an amble, yes, each of his feet operate opposite of the other. Here comes the crab.

Andrew has seen the old man in the laundry room before, in the parking lot, at the mailboxes. When speaking, the old man strokes his white goatee. Andrew has never spoken to the man when he wasn't stroking his white goatee.

As if the man cannot say a word without doing so. Andrew thinks: a mechanism. where one (stroking the beard) activates the other (talking).

Andrew thinks: when listening, I try to stare into his good eye. but more often I wind up following the lazy eye, which bounds about his socket, not very lazy at all. like one of those hand-held games, with pellets. you move around the game and try to get the pellet to rest into the right hole.

Andrew thinks: my childhood was a long time ago.

Andrew watches the old man talk to himself. No. Not that. An earpiece, into which the old man mumbles freely. A telephone, those new kind, the Star

Tick onoo. The future, Andrew wonders, Is there room for me in the future? Is the future out of room already? Booked solid? How will I ever squeeze in?

The old man, hard of hearing, so the mumble becomes loud. Once, between them, a lengthy discussion, the laundry room, the old man unloading, Andrew loading. Andrew only knows his neighbors from the laundry room, from the parking lot, from the mailboxes, from the hallway.

He follows the lazy eye. It relaxes him.

There in the laundry room, they spoke of the current mania in the world, whatever it was that day, vague, elusive statements initially but then the old man narrowed the subject matter to more personal issues when he mentioned his niece, who had just lost her husband to a mental breakdown. The poor beast had been hospitalized and drugged daily in an upstate facility.

His niece, from what the old man could piece together from the few bits of information he'd gathered from relatives he was still on speaking terms with (another story, for another time, how families simply stop speaking to each other, take sides in arguments that go nowhere), had, after returning from a particularly demoralizing visit to see her husband, where the poor beast attempted to rip out his own teeth with his fingers, a bloody mess, half bitten fingertips, gore, and made squealing sounds, the poor beast, spitting blood, and one tooth, while bounding around the visiting room in seizure, off the walls, at one point scrambling up onto a table, pulling off his pants, and lunging desperately (full of rage, his eyes ablaze) at his own penis, with his mouth, his teeth chomping down, his bloody mouth, his bloody hands, his penis rising, far, out into the room, but not, luckily for him, far enough. The old man's niece, shell shocked, returned to her home, quietly made tea, the kettle whistling a lovely off-key F-sharp, sipped with delicacy, and then dragged across her throat a razor blade she'd found at the bottom of the bathroom vanity.

The niece succeeded in losing so much blood that she fell into an arrest, a coma, and had not been heard from since.

Lying in bed day after day, she relied on tubes for breathing, the intake of nutrients, the release of bladder and bowel. It was a sordid tale in which the old man took no relish, despite being cast off from that side of the family. In fact he told the facts as if reading them from the newspaper.

People, is all he said, and folded underwear, rolled socks into balls. The conversation was over when his laundry was all folded, just like that, in mid plot. He left, and took the lazy eye with him.

Now, the old man slides into his sports-car, sleek little convertible. Red. Starts it up, a quiet hum. A whisper.

It floats across the parking lot. The engine coos. Dan's woman's engine purred. The garbage truck lion-roared. Andrew relishes in the thought that everything.

No matter what it is.

Makes a sound.

Has a soul, a place where that sound comes from.

He reaches for his guitar, to make his own sound. He pulls the strap over his head. His fingers move, apart from him, individuals. The fingers glide and bend and pull at strings. He feels slowed down but moving inside. His feet are bare and pink and raw in old carpeting crusty from where paint has spilled and dried.

At the balcony door, glass, and mesh of screen door, the plastic drapes pulled to one side. He plays to an audience of rooftops, clouds, pigeons.

The old man in his sports-car drives past a woman. She is in the middle of the parking lot, elderly, housecoat, slippers. Both her hands grip hard the handles of her walker.

Andrew watches her. What is she doing there?

Quiet, he plays.

Gentle.

Glide, let the fingers glide. Find the notes, without looking, let them find me. See the fret-board, without eyes. Feel it. Play by feel. Watch the woman, don't watch my fingers.

The elderly woman stretches against the walker, by holding onto the handles, and pushing out one leg, then bringing it back, pushing out the other. Exercises?

Doctor's orders?

He shows her, in his office, the doctor.

Like this, he says. And this.

You must exercise your legs, the doctor says, or you will lose them. I will cut them off. I will have no choice. You will have stumps. Do you want stumps?

Andrew is concerned about the woman. She does not belong there, in the middle of the parking lot, clad in a loose housecoat. She's ventured too far. He plays the guitar. Gently, surely. He misses not a note. Full, rich. Easy. Natural. Now, a car.

Its motor a smoker's cough.

Green, older model. Stops for the woman. Slowly, the tires inch.

Andrew thinks: yes. good. her ride.

Her son probably, good. No. The car passes. Not her son. No one.

The woman, stranded.

No more exercise. No more stretch. Her hands hang on to the walker now and her arms shake. She is stranded. She is afraid to move.

The lake, across the street. She stares, lost, at the lake across the street. She concentrates on the geese in their minor activities: flap, splash, plunge. Concentrates, the woman, stares.

Andrew watches her. He plays his guitar.

He is sick to his stomach.

He thinks, he knows.

By playing he keeps her upright. He doesn't understand it, but knows it. He knows it as an absolute. He knows it deep down inside. He knows if he stops playing the guitar, the old woman will fall. He wants to run down there. Wants to take her by the arm. Lead her home, to sit, rest, relax, let her catch her breath, let the fear leave, let the exhaustion. So badly he wants to help her.

But he knows.

When he stops playing, she will fall. He must keep playing the guitar, to hold her up.

If he stops playing.

Even for a moment.

She will fall.

He knows this.

He can't turn a doorknob, handle a key, without removing his hand, without stopping.

So he plays, protects her. But his fingers. The pain in his fingers. He strums now. Missing chords. His fingers ache. Start to go numb. The woman struggles as he struggles, her leg buckles.

Pain surrounds his hand, wrist, shoots up his arm. His shoulder is on fire. His fingers in agony. A disease.

Diagnosed last year. The test for it made him yelp, bite his lip. The needles plunged into fresh skin. Deep, the needles. Thick, jammed into his hand, fleshy palm, and then fingers, web like, in between, while a machine showed readings on a small digital screen. And his hand was a pin-cushion, full of needles jutted in directions, all. Bruising, already.

The doctor, shiny black hair, healthy, cute nose (but no smile Andrew could find despite his excavations for one, as many bitten-lip jokes all failed). Throughout the pain of the needles (thick as cables in his mind), and between the pain of mis-fired jokes, Andrew concentrated on the young doctor's beauty, her dark hair, shiny, dark eyes, to seal his mind off from what was, by then, torture.

You could have smiled, Andrew said to her when they were done. He shook out his hand.

Pay your bill on the way out, she said.

But now Andrew plays his guitar, through the pain. He tells himself: I must keep that old woman standing. there is no pain. there is no pain.

Teeth, gritted.

His fingers numb, missing more strings, can't feel the pick and it drops to the floor. Muffled strums. The pain worse and then worse. With each flaw in his playing, the old woman falters a little. Another leg buckles, her arms shake. She nearly goes down to one knee. So now the obvious: not only must I keep playing, but I must play *well*.

Finally.

A car. Appearing out of nowhere, magic, a miracle, a car backing up, a man jumping out, helps her inside. Great care. Cradling her, her full weight falls against him. He guides her into the passenger seat. Tucks in her arm. Tucks in her leg. Pauses.

A sigh, possibly.

The trunk pops open and the man, much more than half the old woman's age.

    Balding.

    Rickety himself.

    Places (with the same care he gave her) the old woman's walker inside the trunk. Then struggles in behind the steering wheel. Door closes. Motor, the gasp of a cat. The cat drags itself away, leaving a smear of blood.

    Oil.

    Then, only then. Andrew hangs both arms, shakes them out, so the blood might rush back, so the pain might subside.

    Some.

He pulls the guitar up, ducks through the strap, and places it into its stand, tilted.

He walks into the kitchen. Takes out a cutting board and places it on the counter. Removes a large knife from a drawer. Lays his shoulder on the cutting board. Raises the knife into the air.

In the hallway, a conversation. Peek through the eyehole, Andrew, to watch a neighbor and a person he's never seen before. Their mouths move. Their eyes. Their faces change expression in flashes.

One says: I defrosted chicken last night, so there's that, and I think I have *lima beans* in the cupboard but other than that...oh, and some yellow squash, three large bowling pins of them...

The other laughs and repeats the words *bowling pins*.

The first says, laughs too, Well they *look* like bowling pins!

Lima beans! the other says, slap, a knee, chokes, face red.

Those bowling pins, the one says. Taste like a dream after a few minutes in the old George Foreman grill! Some crushed pepper, sea salt, oregano...

George Foreman grill! the other squeals, out of breath, down on one knee, the wall, using the wall to keep from. Oh, I'm gonna pee! I'm gonna pee!

Falling.

The one is a man and the other is a woman.

They disappear inside a door. When they are gone, Andrew. He opens his door.

Inspect the carpeting.

Where a dark spot resembles a map of Texas. And the smell, pungent, overpowering.

Andrew, on all fours, brings his nose to the map. Inhales.

Deep.

Inhales again.

Deep.

His penis juts.

And finds rising within him the urge to lick the map.

He considers the aroma's voluptuousness. His breathing becomes erratic, as he pictures the place it came from. A woman's urine. His erection at full discomfort now.

Arriving at that moment, the old man with the sports-car, cradling in one arm a crisp paper-bag, alcohol bottle inside. He stops. But never really stops. To be precise, he stops walking but his body never stops moving, vibrating. His lazy eye rolls around and around in his head. The pellet game. A marble in a shoebox.

He strokes his goatee. He says to Andrew: did you do that?

No.

What are you doing down there then?

I'm not sure.

It's a woman's pee, the old man says.

How can you be sure?

It is, isn't it?

Andrew says: yes.

Stick your finger in it, the old man says. You know you want to.

It's not my finger that I want to, Andrew says, then abandons the sentence.

The old man stares at Andrew.

The old man walks down the hall and stops. He turns. What's the knife for?

I was going to cut my arm off.

Why?

The pain.

Oh. From a gaggle of keys that jingle, he pulls one out, opens his front door.

Andrew licks the map.

The old man blinks several times, then shuts his door.

Later. Later as a unit of time, a unit of time Andrew understands. Before also. Now. For instance, *Now* there is a knock on Andrew's door. He is naked.

At the door, Greta, her lips tied in the knot of a severe pout, her hair not recently combed. You have no clothes on, she says. Every time I come here, you have no clothes on.

Andrew shrugs.

You have no hair on your chest, do you shave it off?

No. I just have no hair on my chest. Well, there's a little. He looks down at himself, so his chin. Rests. There, see. There's some.

Greta walks up to Andrew. Her hand shakes. Flat, she places her palm to Andrew's chest. The hand lingers, cold, without sensuality. Then, trembling, she pulls the hand back.

She looks at Andrew: one of us has no soul.

She notices: your back is bleeding.

>Again?

>A little.

>It keeps…since the high heel.

>My high heel?

>Yours?

>I've been looking for that.

>How did it get in my bedroom?

>Are you kidding?

>Kidding?

>That's why Pete, when he found out. The ash tray.

>But I thought.

>Everyone thinks.

Now, again. The unit of time. *Now*, Andrew wears jeans, tee shirt. He hears wings, tiny. He crushes them, or tries to, by blinking hard.

Greta on the couch with a glass of water. She wears clothes, what are clothes, a skirt and top, what is a skirt. A top makes sense. It's worn on…top. She is silent. Not silent, her breathing, Andrew hears her breathing, and a small nearly indecipherable click in her throat. Nearly indecipherable. He deciphers it. No, not deciphers, not translates, not defines. He only hears it.

There is something. They are right there, the words. But not yet. Andrew waits. Greta waits. Silence, for real now that the click is gone, now that the breathing, when there is so much silence that the silence is a noise. He is confused and understands it is only a matter of time before silence, any prolonged silence, will swallow him whole. He will disappear inside it forever.

The water. The glass. She sips.

I did it.

Did what?

Put the pistol to his head.

Andrew watches her.

She says, I held it to his forehead while he slept.

While he slept?

Yes. I had drawn on him with a marker.

A marker?

Yes. So I would know where to shoot.

You made a target?

Yes. It was black.

The pistol?

No. Well, yes. The pistol was black, is black. But I mean the marker. I drew on his forehead, that spot between the eyes, the famous spot. *Right between the eyes.* An X. Like X marks the spot.

Did you fire it?

The marker?

No the pistol.

No.

Andrew thinks: okay.

I laid it on his chest. I wanted him to know I could have.

Is he awake?

I don't think so.

Are you going back there?

I don't think so.

Do you want to stay here?

I don't think so.

Greta shuts the door behind her. A quiet whoosh. He forgets, he remembers, someone was just here, but who. Who was just here? What was said? There is a high-heel shoe on his coffee-table, on its side.

Later, the unit of time. Not Before, the unit of time. *Now.*

Right *now* police are in Andrew's building.

They question the female cousins who live on the first floor and find out that Greta had once been in a mental hospital, the army, and deeply involved with the actress Darryl Hannah.

The police leave.

Andrew is not sure what is happening.

On his balcony he reads Rien Ne Va Plus. The writer is dead, he thinks, the person who wrote this is dead. Andrew sees Pete walk across the parking lot, over broken glass. Hunched and tip-toe. Andrew watches this from his balcony, high up. He feels very far away.

Also: Pete is smiling.

Also: a white bandage, in the space.

In the space between. That X, covering it. Andrew notices the smile. It is not a smile. It is a grimace. Andrew wonders if Pete is off to bury bodies in a garbage dump, or dig them up, play music from the car radio, and dance with them. Andrew thinks this could happen. Pete stops sudden. He looks up at Andrew. Pete squints in the sun. He waves. Andrew waves. It's not Pete. That's not Pete, Andrew thinks. That's Pete. Is that Pete?

Andrew decides not to talk to anyone any more. It's too dangerous. People are bombs, and when he meets one he has no idea how far along the fuse is. Will it be weeks before the bomb explodes? Days? Minutes? Any second now? It's all too much of a chance to take.

Andrew thinks: yes. it's for the best. I'm off people now. people are an addiction.

I will quit my job. I don't go there any more anyway.

I will have all my groceries delivered (just leave them at the door).

I will never answer my door again, pick up a phone, check my mail.

A word. Just a word. There are a lot of words. How can all those words mean something different. There should just be one word. One word in the human language. Human language should consist of just one word.

But what word?
The word fuck?

River?

Tumor?

Maybe two words.

Yes. No.

Pete has driven off. It is Pete. It's not Pete. Was that just Pete? A book in Andrew's lap. He thinks: I can be very quiet. I don't grumble or sigh or cough or sneeze or read out loud. no, when I read I am invisible. if I just keep reading, I will be invisible, and everything will be okay.

Andrew's neighbor, she, her cell phone. On her balcony, one below his, Andrew hears her. Into the phone she says: I don't like to do things I don't like to do. I am trying to live a life without obligations. it's that new way we were talking about, and if I go to the funeral it will strictly be out of obligation, and that defeats everything. what am I doing with my life if the first time this comes up my big plan crumbles so easily?

Silence.

While, presumably.

She listens to the person on the other end talk.

Andrew goes inside. He goes down for the mail. The postcards, from his friend in California, gathered now in his hand. His feet move. Over black-top that has been chewed up, clawed at. Over grass. Over wood. Over sand.

The first post-card, a Max Ernst painting on the front, on the back in black ink scrawl: piano bar in Angel Town.

The next one: Portland is Hippie Paris.

The next: it's true, you can be a good person without being a perfect person.

The last (so far): the Rage Express has stopped at Junction Hills, Colorado. We smokers have to stick together, they put us out in the pouring rain, the blazing sunshine. They hurry us up. Try to leave us behind. Constant battle.

Andrew's friend has been gone forty-four days. Now a train, heading back across the country, east, home.

Friends take turns being each other's hero. This time it is Andrew's friend's turn. Andrew's friend is Andrew's hero, for:

Leaving for California in order to live a life of inspiration and beauty, fleeing the mundane, the prison of mind-numbing activities he found himself chained to.

Employment.

Schedules.

Sobriety.

A woman he does not love.

A son that is not his.

Andrew receives telephone dispatches from different parts of the country. Colorado. Montana. The deserts and cities of Nevada, three thousand miles take a long time.

Each dispatch contains a little more dread in the voice. As the time-change shrinks from three hours in California to two in Colorado to one in Chicago, so does shrink Andrew's friend's enthusiasm for life. Andrew's friend is devolving back into the depressed manic personality he was before he left.

Andrew walks to his car. He has no intention of going anywhere. He leans on the back bumper. He glances up toward his neighbor's balcony, the one he overheard on the phone. She is not there. He walks across the street, and then down to the water. People swim.

People lie on blankets spread out over the sand. Some, umbrellas, stuck. There is a tent.

Down at the mouth of the ocean Andrew stands in the wind. In his hand the postcards, flip, one at a time, into the froth. The thick cardboard could be baseball cards: picture on front, vital statistics on back.

Andrew thinks:

What kind of ballplayer would I be? A slugger with an iron glove, who plods pitifully around the bases? Pound the ball off the wall time after time, only to get thrown out at second base trying to claim the double such a long, hard hit ball deserves?

A slick-fielding middle infielder with lightning fast reflexes, superb baseball instincts, knowledge of the game's glorious past, a knack for the hit-n-run, a talent for laying down a bunt in a crucial situation, but no pop in my bat? I could steal a base, tag up and go from first to second on a medium-range fly ball to center (not a common occurrence).

Twice in my career I had stolen home to win a game, once in extra innings, in the playoffs. I understood the nuances of the game and would one day be a top-flight manager.

Or possibly a bench player, living for that one great moment of pitch-hitting legend? Or a middle-reliever with a mid-range arm surviving on an 86-mile an hour fastball and a truck load of guts. I would shuttle back and forth from the minors until I finally stuck at the age of thirty-three?

Or a career minor leaguer, who never even got a whiff of the Bigs, yet unselfish, and pass along his wisdom to the younger players, some half his age?

Yes.

Andrew decides.

That last one, that's the one. A gentleman loser, a winner only to himself. Toss, fling, the postcards. Feed the great mouth of time and breath. Feed the ocean.

With, word.

Art.

Thought.

Regret.

Sublime remorse.

His neighbor, the one who had been on the phone. She stares long and hard at the ocean, her bottom stuck down in the sand, her hands behind her propping her up, legs outstretched. She has long red hair, the wind blows it back, a flag snapping in the wind, claiming sadness. Andrew.

Sits next to her.

Andrew wonders what makes people sad. Happy. Certainly, outside influences decide mood. Also, it comes from inside. Which one am I, Andrew wonders.

Should I keep thinking about this?

Will it get me anywhere?

He takes a nap. He wakes up and takes a shower and reads from Pornografia and takes a nap.

He wakes up, puts his shoes on. He goes outside. Across the street is the lake. The geese are out. They wade and honk. Make trickling sounds. On a bench, in the grass, a tree, large rocks, the sun on his shoulders, hot, top of his head, hot. His mind, his memory, pushes out certain images from the past.

His mind pushes out...

San Francisco, North Beach, Andrew and Andrew's friend, at the bar. His friend, the look of a longshoreman just off the boat. Mangled hair and face, sad drowsy eyes. His voice no emotion, no concern. Whiskey in small glasses on the bar in front of them.

Seven in the morning.

Not crowded.

That guy who comes in every morning, suit, slicked hair. End of the bar, stands erect. Orange juice and vodka. Slams the drink, slams his fist. VIET NAM!

STILL! STILL!

THEY CHANGE THE NAMES THAT'S ALL! THEY CAN CALL IT THIS-A-STAN AND THAT-A-STAN BUT IT'S STILL VIET NAM TO ME!

He finishes his drink and leaves.

The bartender, white hair, Mark Twain, disheveled in old black vest. He says, Here.

To Andrew's friend.

A twenty dollar bill.

You left too much last night. You wandered off. I figured it was for more drinks and you were coming back. You never came back.

Andrew through the double doors. Sunshine. Busy street. California. Andrew stretches, looks around. Activity, everybody is everywhere at once, moving, moving. Feet and clothes and heads and eyes. Arms swing. Hips swerve. I am moving. I am not moving. But I am moving. Inside, I am moving fast.

People walk by.

Girls, women he means, wear boots, high up. Almost all of them. Long straight hair, pretty lips, and boots.

High up.

Trends. What are *trends*?

Andrew wonders what is popular, why is it popular, how did it get popular, how does anything get popular? who decides? What is moody? What does aloof mean? A girlfriend, once. She told him he had a ghost heart. She said his lips tasted like sun poisoning.

Andrew didn't know the meaning. He didn't ask or say don't go. He watched her put clothes and picture frames in a suitcase.

She left in the night, right in the middle. Andrew stood in a corner, watched her. He had no hands and the shadows kept up all illusion. Andrew trusted shadows. He trusted quiet rooms, dark corners. Downstairs, framed in the doorway. She said, You try to cram yourself inside your head, but you can never fit all of you. There is always part of you hanging out, arm, leg, idea, fault. I don't know how to deal with pieces of you when it's a different piece every day.

Andrew's friend, finally. Emerges through the bar doors, squint. Jesus, the sun, he murmurs, hand, up to his face, palm, toward the day. Head turned.

Andrew says really?

Yes, really.

One punch like that?

Yes and right to the floor.

You're pissed because he took your hat, but you laughed.

I laughed but it wasn't funny.

We can't go in there again.

Andrew's friend points his finger at Andrew, a gun, and goes. Bang.

Andrew's friend says, Yes we can.

We can go anywhere we want.

Andrew and his friend, *their feet their only carriage.* Walk and walk, ten miles, twenty, a day. More some days. Nooks, crannies, nestle in and learn, dig in, dig in, find out about a city. Crawl inside people.

Live there, not visit.

Talk.

Love people, like them. *Courage,* Andrew thinks, would be a good line too.

At the lake now, the memory over, bench, geese, sun, hot on his shoulders and top of head. Andrew thinks to himself: I shouldn't be here. where should I be?

Em, faraway, her body, from Andrew's body. This long is too long. This bothers him. He calls her. She says a lot, there's a lot. On my mind.

A lot huh?

Yes Andrew.

Like what?

Well.

But not me. I'm not on your mind.

My art, Andrew.

Yes.

I'm learning so much.

Okay then.

Don't be like this, Andrew.

Learn then.

Andrew? Andrew. Andrew...

Andrew's balcony, in the sunshine, sunshine warm on his legs, his calves, tender, they ache but like sex, like orgasm. The ache is good. A different feeling than he has had. Squeezing the tired out of his legs. He looks for blood. No, because the sun, a knife-WOUND and not a KNIFE.

On the next balcony over, a dog. A puppy, content, cute. Car pulls in and the puppy, abrupt, alerted, barks his young dog high-pitched baby bark. His eyes are fresh. He learns with each day, with each minute. Now up on all fours, fully extended, tail wagging in circles. The tail stops, a switch flicked, and the tail, motionless and rigid, high in the air, is at the same height as the snout, which is pushed forward and out, tip to tail. He has no idea why he's interested in that car. He is simply interested in it.

Andrew says, Em.

Yes?

When can I kiss you again?

When it stops raining, she says.

It falls hard and steady, this Dutch rain. Amsterdam, and midnight rescues the evening. Dark hue, colorless color. Every cobblestone a rain-slicked face alive in the darkness. Indefinable. Indigestible, this food of life. Let it sit, then, Andrew thinks.

Lighting matches in my gut. Growling at the bottom of
my throat. Bathing in my tongue's juices Andrew
thinks: if I swallow this moment, will there ever be
another one just like it?

Three of them. All day, Red Light District, all
night. The younger one must find that shop from
earlier, for a bong, he coveted. It is imperative to his
existence. He will not survive without it. The mission,
though, is to find, not what is found.

Andrew had told him buy it now, we'll never
remember this place. The younger one said, It's too
early. I don't want to carry it around with me all day.
We'll find it.

So, for an hour, for over that, hours, the younger
one searched for the shop, in the dark, among the
closed shops, was there really a head shop, was it
hallucination, ghost, dream? Duck down wrong alleys,
repeat steps, start, stop, it's this way, no, wait, this
looks familiar, does this look familiar? I feel familiar.
This is familiar. Are you familiar? Is this familiar?

Familiar.

Familiar.

Is that a word? It doesn't look like a word. Is
familiar a word I'm familiar with, Andrew thinks.

Determined now more than ever, convinced he
is on the right trail, the younger one leads the way
while the woman and Andrew follow, rain, slash and
thrash and drops harder with every step.

Soon, the woman and Andrew come up with a
strategy. Avoid the rain. Doorways. Run from one to
the next. Bars, closed newspaper shops, pipe shops,
erotic clothes store, music store with instruments
strung up in the window, any overhang.

Will do.

Each new doorway, they revel in, happy exhausted grins, hair matted to foreheads, their clothes drip water, refuge from the pelting rain. They remain there.

Pant.

Giddy.

A few moments to gather themselves.

Then run to the next. In theory, this can go on indefinitely. The younger one has no strategy, or interest in one, keeps up an increasing speed down the middle of the road. His duty is clear: find that shop. Still in shouting distance, from time to time, one of them, yells, out, and then the return.

But fainter and then fainter, before, finally, nothing can be heard.

Still, the younger one treks through the murk and mess of a stormy night in Europe, still the younger one, the dark wet dot of his existence is well up ahead. The fuzz and mystery of time and place. Soon that vanishes, too. And there is only darkness. Colorless color.

At a certain doorway, the woman and Andrew, enough. They look at each other. Exhaustion is no theory, and, without language, verbal at least, they agree. Andrew.

Pushes his shoulder against the door, and they fall inside the bar.

Crowded – no, hardly anyone inside. Music, blues, scratches from a beat-up jukebox. Bar top worn down, human skin, rubbed raw. Walls hover. A place.

To dissolve.

A place.

To sit quiet in corners with old book, cognac, storm outside.

A place.

To hide.

From tomorrow.

From yesterday.

From the hunters in life. From the trappers looking for the trapped.

Andrew slides onto a stool. The woman onto the stool next to him. They drip puddles at their feet.

The bartender, tall, seven feet, missing one. An arm. An American, from Boston. Tequila, the woman says.

One Arm pours three.

My wife that cunt she made me a coward. To run away from your home is to break your own heart. Boston is a long way from here, but at least here the ghosts don't run at you with their teeth bared.

Tequila, the bottle as big as a pig.

Head.

The spout, the snout.

Pool table in back, nicked up, gouged, stories soaked in, stained, beer, blood. The woman breaks, and billiard balls scatter over the green felt, rush away from each other, before, a few at least, huddle together in corners.

Against the wall, beer bottles, empties, stacked to a pyramid. The pyramid an accomplishment, a structure.

There is a smell. And flies, bloated and slow. Thick, sticky chunks of air.

Slam faces.

Orbit and surrender.

Bartender shoots one handed, sinks his ball. His eyes shine. He motions to the bathrooms. Last month, a man. He was dead in there for three days.

Three days?

We didn't know what to do with him.

What happened?

I don't know. One day he was here, one day he wasn't. Like everybody else. It wasn't my shift. I came in and he wasn't here.

The younger one walks in. Does he have the bong? Soaked to the bone. Wet teeth and water logged.

Em. She tells Andrew: anytime you want. I don't care.

But you said the rain, when the rain stops.

Andrew watches her, as a stranger now, for a moment, then the moment is gone, and her familiarity rushes back. Now she is his mother, for a moment. A girl he knew in high school, for a moment. A death he read about in the newspapers. She is all these.

Em, confused. She starts to say, but doesn't. Turns away from. Turns back. Stares at him. And, finally, mired in an old sadness between them: Andrew stop it, stop zoning out, you scare me.

Andrew says, Who are you?

Em, scrunching her face, a teacher, a parent, annoyed at her children. That's a big question. Why do you only ask big questions?

Andrew says: no. really. do I know you?

Andrew, barely audible, has become a thought in his own head now, escaped entirely into that. He thinks out loud. My father, when I hit him with the car. In the hospital they asked me questions because he couldn't answer them, and then I couldn't answer them. I didn't know where he lived, worked. I forgot his name.

Em says quietly, Andrew. She strokes his hair.

Teddy was here, he says. Staying with me, he comes and goes, his wife, she told him never come back, I said stay, what are brothers for?

In her panties, she, and tee shirt, smokes at the window. Inside the apartment, her body. Outside, her hand with the cigarette. And the smoke, unwelcome, barges in past bare emotions. She thinks all those buildings, all those people in them.

Andrew walks up behind her, his hand on her back.

A brush, barely.

Of fingers.

Flesh.

Now his chin on her shoulder, his stare right behind hers, aligned. She sucks on the cigarette, blows it out, a way to let.

Time.

Dismantle.

Love.

Andrew on his balcony, alone, this a simple action, one of many, one of few. He drifts in and out of memories, now, here and not here, somewhere, but where? The sun, in denims, a little boy, runs behind a cluster of bruised clouds, chase raindrops with a tongue, a tin can. In a less frenzied delirium, in a more, fat, succulent, explode in the street.

If ink, they would spell out names, old criminals he shared time and space with. The water keeps coming, the sky an endless, an endless, what, he isn't sure, except for endless, and the names, at first, dilute, as ink will when up against water, runs, and then gone. But never gone.

One more memory, the last. Is this my life, passing, my eyes? Is this my parade-march off the edge of the world? My world. Existence, mine, about to, the void, a, into.

Plunge.

Vanish.

Dissolve and cease.

If I am dying, what am I dying from? If I am losing, my mind, where is it going? If I have lost it, what IS this I am in? Where am I speaking from?

Close friends, only. Eight, at the table set with care, in the dining room. In the corner, an armoire, glass doors, and inside, crystal glasses, fine china. Above their heads a chandelier, miniature, intricate. A painting, centered on the wall, depict a family at dinner.

In a vase, fresh flowers.

Burning at various points of the room, candles, scented.

The woman from Queens, lives in New Jersey now, all day spent, the stove. Her food a rush to the senses, a fever. Italian. Wine.

Her husband, The Fireman, big, broad, gregarious. Teller of stories.

Laughter at the table. Everyone.

When Andrew laughs hard, often, hiccups, a bad and worsening spell, and an old issue, arrive with pomp and circumstance, a parade of minute disasters.

He is forced to the kitchen, convulse the whole short trip, his agony brings more laughter, to the crowd, to the table. They spit up their drinks. Their faces, red, to burst. They lose control.

He can't stop! It's every time! It's *every* time!

Laugh so hard that something, food, snot chunk, flies from the nose, while another laughs so hard she snorts, covers her mouth, laughs harder, now at herself, the table explodes with laughter, tears flow.

The woman from Queens follows Andrew into the kitchen, desperate attempt to keep her composure. But, no. Instead, enormous the smile, bubble to the surface, thwart her efforts to keep a face not crooked with laughter.

Andrew attempts. Yes, really tries, to talk between hiccups, stutter, words cut in half, near burps, gulps, tears stream. He pleads for the straw.

Which she retrieves, the straw, kept specifically for Andrew, from a kitchen drawer.

She readies a full glass of water.

The straw, Andrew places, sideways in his mouth, a dog his bone. Drinks down the water, fast, is the point. Yes, water dribbles down his chin, but no. No time for.

Manners. There is no time to spare, or, yes, the whole procedure must be repeated. And more hiccups, stutter, words cut in half, burps, gulps, tears. His throat hurts. A headache from.

It has to be now, the straw, the water.

The secret, the activating factor, is how the water goes down, the air-flow in the throat. The straw changes the dynamic, the path.

This carnival act works nine times out of ten. And the hiccups, as with any torture at some point, stop.

It works this time.

The woman from Queens watches, careful, her palms out in front of her, careful, picture a cake in the oven. Well?

Andrew breathes, hiccup free. Relief. His cheeks drenched with tears, his shirt-front dark from water dribbled, eyes red, wet. Gasp, slight.

Andrew re-enters the dining room. His friends are quiet, somber, faceless, blasé, a zombie lounge, a funeral. Finally the man from upstate New York, in that way of his, his sublime humor, more than dead-pan, tells a joke, old, a favorite.

Yes, Andrew, damnit, he, laughs without control. And the hiccups, again, the spasms, again. The woman from Queens moans, hysterical, despondent. I'll get the straw!

The women, the woman from Queens, and the other woman from Queens, have taken a corner of the table for themselves, where, their mothers, they discuss, grope for, answers. Source of pain for them both, their mothers. Andrew hears less and less of their conversation until it is gone completely from his consciousness.

Instead he has slow and sure been absorbed into another conversation. The men. The Fireman (husband of the woman from Queens). The man from upstate New York (the husband of the other woman from Queens). And the Man of Many Women.

Are involved in their own conversation, world events, which, yes, bore Andrew. Instead, it is the sound of their voices, each different from the other, which draws Andrew in, different so, when spoken one over the other, create.

Song.

Music.

Eloquence in the phrasing, jazz, spontaneous. Formless. One breaks in where another leaves off, or has not quite left off, right before the leaving off, so a fluidity is created, a handing off, the piano hands off to the horn, the horn takes off. The bass and drums of a secondary conversation, in the background, and the group is tight. Melodies soar over a locked-in rhythm energy.

By now, Andrew has no idea what is being said.

Soon, the man from upstate New York whispers *Twenty-two*, his hands in front of him, mimic, cup two grocery-store melons, bouncing, his hands, eyebrows raised, mouth forms to whistle (but doesn't).

More details follow, nothing terribly. Crude. His secretary, a secret. Even the word secretary. Secret ary. He has touched her only with the groping hands of

desire, fantasy, but his wife, she, will consider those
hands flesh.

After dinner, the party, outside, is moved, to the patio.
Tables, chairs, long, large, porch-roof covers every
head, cake and coffee, candles, cigars, liqueurs, coi fish
in the fish pond, crickets. The fireman puffs on a
stogie, leans back. He says the netting, over the pond,
that's why, because that fucking bird, I don't know
what he was. Hon?

His wife makes a face. Oh God I don't know.

The fireman says because of that bastard, he
swoops down from the trees, a monster, plucks his
catch for the day. Dinner for the bastard. Later, he
comes back for dessert. It's gotten to where I'm
restocking the pond every other week, well, we, right
Hon? Those little sons of bitches aren't cheap!

Does the net work?

Yes and no. One morning we found a hole in the
netting. Could have been squirrels though, or the dog. I
keep trying to count the fish. But they move around too
quick.

His wife says she saw it, the bird, wingspan,
like, like.

A terror dackle.

A what?

Terror dackle.

Everyone laughs, except the fireman's wife.

What? I'm from Queens, what do I know about
dinosaur birds? Fuck youse all. It was a big frickin bird,
alright!

Andrew isn't sure how it starts. The Man of Many Women is gone, to meet his new girlfriend, a dance place forty five minutes away, rolls his eyes as he leaves, says old, I'm old, can't even get out of this chair without all my bones snapping, how am I going to dance tonight?

Two neighbors arrive, women. Around the table, dodge mosquitoes, even though.

Those special candles, in a tub. Burn. Everyone glows dim in the strange light given off.

The dog.

Seven pounds.

Splashes in the fish pond.

Conversations split, divide, find form in small groups. Separate. People in a small area, miles apart. The woman from Queens, speaks to the two neighbors, stops talking. It's abrupt. She makes a face at Andrew, who, Andrew, has been quiet in the shadows, murmuring.

An exchange, less than civil.

What did you say?

Nothing, I.

Did you just say—?

Wasn't talking.

That I.

To you.

The woman from Queens says Andrew, your girl, halfway across the country, this girl of yours, what does she love, what is there of you to love?

Andrew, dissolving.

The man from upstate New York, drunk, grins, slumped in his chair, joyous, his wife, who resents his good time, who always resents his happiness, because

it is a guiltless joy, his, a joy with no merit, in her view,
a joy he does not deserve, her husband, who works a
distance from home to evade her, and whose
happiness, his, is a mirror, an unflattering reflection
back at her, a reminder, constant, that the happiness
which so easily invades her husband's being, so easily
evades hers. Evade, again. She is a sadness, that
emotion's walking epitome, sadness and self-hatred
personified, in the true meaning of that overused word,
personified, sadness with a face, not a sad face, but.
Sadness, itself, *with* a face.

She scolds her husband, attempts to peel, with a
long and honed fingernail, no, with her searing hate-
filled eye instead, the good feeling from him. She tells
him don't, don't drink, you diminish yourself when you
drink. You diminish me.

The fireman's wife says Andrew, your woman,
you're always telling us, your clothes, she rips them off.

No, that's not what I.

She talks to the dog, she said it was your
mother.

That was once.

You were not born right.

Andrew murmurs, believes he has vanished. His
outline.

Though.

Remains.

And the words, hateful, whistle through him.

The remark is made: *Is marriage, as I have always
feared, a domination of one over the other? A contest, to
be won and lost?*

The fireman's wife says there has been a death in her belly.

Moonlight makes dim monsters, and candles, and water, trickling, snap of mosquitoes in the bug-zapper, the seven pound dog alert in the grass that comes up to its belly, its paws wet, the crickets, the night, the night, the explosion of silence.

Rain is an exponential event, minor, a simple equation of nature and science, and not a miracle, as poets and other dreamers, often, bear witness to, no, the rain, multiplies, by the moment. At first there is more sky than rain, and the eye must concentrate in order to find it, the rain. But soon there is more rain than sky, and the eye must concentrate, to find it, the sky.

Andrew, his balcony. In the chair he watches his feet. Splattered. In the parking lot, cars are pelted. Loud noises that make him sleepy. This goes on. Also: a safe feeling. Also:

The spine, warm.

A human mind, often, a weapon, to gore and puncture, slice and stab, to self-inflict, but also to soothe, elixir, cool wash of hand-made cloth along the body. Silk, to wrap bones in before transporting.

Losing friends is not the same as willingly giving them up. Often, a person or persons will enter each other's life or lives at a certain time for a certain reason. Staying together beyond that reason is a mistake.

The weather, beastly, no, a haven, remembers his skin.
The cold is comfort. The rawness is familiar, the sting
is welcome. Andrew becomes more and more drowsy.
He lets his eyes drop.

At a diner, a waitress, older, career waitress, her hair
the length of a younger woman's, unruly like a younger
woman's, but brittle, not soft, like a younger woman's,
her face, crags, her skin a rough terrain, blotch, stretch,
droop her eyes, and bags, swollen, red, stockings
clumped, medical shoes, she pulls Andrew into the
kitchen. The kitchen is loud, hot, busy with waiters,
cooks. In her hand, papers, a new story. Pulled from an
oversized purse with a padlock on it. The purse is
white, the padlock gold, not a padlock, a heavy clasp.
No, it's a padlock. There's a key.

Outside, by the dumpster, she reads the story,
her voice moves in the air. Hair in her eyes. She pulls
hair from her face, it falls back, she pulls hair. She reads
with one eye looking.

Around.

Furtive.

Her voice alive, now, when Andrew listens, her
voice is alive.

The dumpster. Moonlight crashes to the ground
around them. She reads pages and pages.

She stops, stares, big red eyes, lopsided sacks of
sight. She stops, watches Andrew, for, reaction, for
sprouted wings, for jet-packs, diamonded—

Andrew holds out his arms. She falls into them,
lays her head on his shoulder. They are like that a
while.

Moonlight.

Dumpster.

She hugs tight, tighter, tries to squeeze herself inside him.

A busboy comes out, dumps large rubber bucket. Heaves black rubber mats with factory-made holes in them, over railing, then a hose, hoses down the mats. He may have seen Andrew and the waitress or he may not have seen Andrew and the waitress.

Soon he is gone, the water has splashed, runs down the blacktop, and the mats are left to drip over the railings.

Theodore has not been around in a while. Andrew thinks, I hit him with the car, right. Is that the one?

Andrew thinks: why did I go to that diner?

Because I go there every week, every week she reads me a story. He remembers his childhood, when she used to paint.

Andrew, his balcony. It's late. But voices. Up the street. The summer-rentals. Friday night parties. The voices, light, happy, laughter joyous, unimpeded, by sadness, lingering.

Pure.

Pure.

Pure.

A scotch now fills his hand, the glass, his fingers know what to do. Standing, leans his weight against the railing, the weight of many psychological items, memory, regret. Hang both hands over, cupped around his drink. He almost feels good. Nearly but not nearly enough, non-conflicted. It will do, he thinks. I'll take it.

He doesn't take a shower. He doesn't take a nap. The voices up the street, light, happy.

Pure.

He stays up all night, outside, the balcony, lounged in the patio chair, his legs.

Sprawled, and sipping.

Scotch.

The bottle sloshes but the sound is small, barely there. Not much left, a corner maybe, when the bottle tilts. Dawn. Night leaves graceful down the road, jacket slung over one shoulder.

A reverie, unfurled. The flag of every place at once.

Now, the sun, beginning. It will be a while, still, until it holds up the sky. It is still.

Climbing. I am still.

Climbing, he thinks. It will be a while.

Before I hold myself up.

Inside his apartment, there. Again. Yet.

The canvas.

Blank.

The chair, the folding kind, the brush, its whisker ends mangled past the point. But that is the point.

Precision is reliable. Can be duplicated. But.

Imperfection is.

Once. Cannot be.

Replicated.

One, by one, oozes of paint he will need, and squeeze small globs onto the plate.

Mixing, now. He knows it now, he knows the blend. How much, how little, where, and where else. Stroke here. There. Rub. Now with a finger. Finally, finally. But not finally. Not at all – it's all wrong.

A disaster.

Fuck!

Fuck fuck fuck fuck fuck fuck fuck fuck!

Fury, he hurls the plate with paint on it at the balcony door. His face feels stretched in ways it has never been before. He experiences pangs of failure, rip through his insides, buzz-saw.

Splatter, splatter, the glass door. The plate sticks in place. The paint, but. Runs down the glass pane, slow and sickening.

A death.

Andrew, his chest. Heaves. Air sucks violently in and out through mouth and nose. He decides.

Leave it, his anger tells him.

Fuck it, his disgust says.

It's over. Whatever is inside me is still inside me. Will always be inside me. I cannot release it. There, hear it, scratching at the walls, scratching from inside. Forever, now, that scratching. It can't get out. It will not get out. I will never get it out. The vision that haunts, is trapped forever now, inside me. I am trapped, forever now, inside me. I am its prison, and it is mine. I am my prison.

Andrew sleeps, hours. His dreams possess no consequence, and, he, Andrew, remembers nothing. He sleeps lashed, as if to, the bed. His sleep is struggle, to free himself.

He wakes. Limps to the toilet, the sound of water.

Liberated.

Splash and.

Sizzle.

Stumble, sore. Into the living room. There, the balcony door. On the glass, baked in the sun...

His gray!

Excited, Andrew roots around for his brush. Where is it! Where is it! Andrew, he, frantic, pulls out brushes, and tosses, pulls out rags, coffee cans, tosses, over shoulder, and tosses.

Where is it! Where is it!

Fuck!

Fuck!

Fuck!

Then, there, finally! There! In his hand, now! Between fingers. Smears, first, the glass. Then adds three.

Dark.

Gray.

Splotches.

Precise in size, shade, depth. Their geography accurate, a map. Then, with frantic care, removes his face to reveal his face, peels back the stuck-on paper plate. The red arrives, somehow, from a thought, desperate, fleeting, a vision, a visual, a quick blurred action, over skin, the pelt of, a wrist, an accident, an incident, a memory, a precision, a truth, one last truth, a wild string crawls into the painting.

Andrew stands back, afraid it will attack him, hoping it will attack him.

Upright, he, Andrew, stands. Straight! Erect!

His eyes wet and bulge!

The painting on the glass door, exact, to the painting in his head. Free now! It's free now! I'm free now! It's out!

Tremble, shiver.

Heat and cold. He, Andrew, releases the breath he has been holding since birth. The dark bubble inside him. He is lightness now. The struggle, gone. His torment now a bursting garden of flowers. His strength drains because he no longer needs strength. He no longer needs love. He no longer needs life. The painting, the vision! Realized! Realized! The elusive dream every artist, tortured by, is his now. His greatest accomplishment is the map to his inner peace. His head clears. Blinding light. Blinding light. Blinding light, and, in a precise portion of time, the floor, rises.

To meet him.

Joseph Musso Jr. is also the author of the novel-in-stories
I Was Never Cool. He lives in NJ.